CITY OF VICE

(An Ava Gold Mystery—Book Six)

BLAKE PIERCE

Blake Pierce

Blake Pierce is the USA Today bestselling author of the RILEY PAGE mystery series, which includes seventeen books. Blake Pierce is also the author of the MACKENZIE WHITE mystery series, comprising fourteen books; of the AVERY BLACK mystery series, comprising six books; of the KERI LOCKE mystery series, comprising five books; of the MAKING OF RILEY PAIGE mystery series, comprising six books; of the KATE WISE mystery series, comprising seven books; of the CHLOE FINE psychological suspense mystery, comprising six books; of the JESSIE HUNT psychological suspense thriller series, comprising twenty six books; of the AU PAIR psychological suspense thriller series, comprising three books; of the ZOE PRIME mystery series, comprising six books; of the ADELE SHARP mystery series, comprising sixteen books, of the EUROPEAN VOYAGE cozy mystery series, comprising six books; of the LAURA FROST FBI suspense thriller, comprising eleven books; of the ELLA DARK FBI suspense thriller, comprising fourteen books (and counting); of the A YEAR IN EUROPE cozy mystery series, comprising nine books, of the AVA GOLD mystery series, comprising six books (and counting); of the RACHEL GIFT mystery series, comprising ten books (and counting); of the VALERIE LAW mystery series, comprising nine books (and counting); of the PAIGE KING mystery series, comprising eight books (and counting); of the MAY MOORE mystery series, comprising eleven books (and counting); the CORA SHIELDS mystery series, comprising five books (and counting); of the NICKY LYONS mystery series, comprising five books (and counting), and of the new CAMI LARK mystery series, comprising five books (and counting).

An avid reader and lifelong fan of the mystery and thriller genres, Blake loves to hear from you, so please feel free to visit www.blakepierceauthor.com to learn more and stay in touch.

ISBN: 978-1-0943-8006-3

BOOKS BY BLAKE PIERCE

CAMI LARK MYSTERY SERIES
JUST ME (Book #1)
JUST OUTSIDE (Book #2)
JUST RIGHT (Book #3)
JUST FORGET (Book #4)
JUST ONCE (Book #5)

NICKY LYONS MYSTERY SERIES
ALL MINE (Book #1)
ALL HIS (Book #2)
ALL HE SEES (Book #3)
ALL ALONE (Book #4)
ALL FOR ONE (Book #5)

CORA SHIELDS MYSTERY SERIES
UNDONE (Book #1)
UNWANTED (Book #2)
UNHINGED (Book #3)
UNSAID (Book #4)
UNGLUED (Book #5)

MAY MOORE SUSPENSE THRILLER
NEVER RUN (Book #1)
NEVER TELL (Book #2)
NEVER LIVE (Book #3)
NEVER HIDE (Book #4)
NEVER FORGIVE (Book #5)
NEVER AGAIN (Book #6)
NEVER LOOK BACK (Book #7)
NEVER FORGET (Book #8)
NEVER LET GO (Book #9)
NEVER PRETEND (Book #10)
NEVER HESITATE (Book #11)

PAIGE KING MYSTERY SERIES

THE GIRL HE PINED (Book #1)
THE GIRL HE CHOSE (Book #2)
THE GIRL HE TOOK (Book #3)
THE GIRL HE WISHED (Book #4)
THE GIRL HE CROWNED (Book #5)
THE GIRL HE WATCHED (Book #6)
THE GIRL HE WANTED (Book #7)
THE GIRL HE CLAIMED (Book #8)

VALERIE LAW MYSTERY SERIES
NO MERCY (Book #1)
NO PITY (Book #2)
NO FEAR (Book #3)
NO SLEEP (Book #4)
NO QUARTER (Book #5)
NO CHANCE (Book #6)
NO REFUGE (Book #7)
NO GRACE (Book #8)
NO ESCAPE (Book #9)

RACHEL GIFT MYSTERY SERIES
HER LAST WISH (Book #1)
HER LAST CHANCE (Book #2)
HER LAST HOPE (Book #3)
HER LAST FEAR (Book #4)
HER LAST CHOICE (Book #5)
HER LAST BREATH (Book #6)
HER LAST MISTAKE (Book #7)
HER LAST DESIRE (Book #8)
HER LAST REGRET (Book #9)
HER LAST HOUR (Book #10)

AVA GOLD MYSTERY SERIES
CITY OF PREY (Book #1)
CITY OF FEAR (Book #2)
CITY OF BONES (Book #3)
CITY OF GHOSTS (Book #4)
CITY OF DEATH (Book #5)
CITY OF VICE (Book #6)

A YEAR IN EUROPE

A MURDER IN PARIS (Book #1)
DEATH IN FLORENCE (Book #2)
VENGEANCE IN VIENNA (Book #3)
A FATALITY IN SPAIN (Book #4)

ELLA DARK FBI SUSPENSE THRILLER
GIRL, ALONE (Book #1)
GIRL, TAKEN (Book #2)
GIRL, HUNTED (Book #3)
GIRL, SILENCED (Book #4)
GIRL, VANISHED (Book 5)
GIRL ERASED (Book #6)
GIRL, FORSAKEN (Book #7)
GIRL, TRAPPED (Book #8)
GIRL, EXPENDABLE (Book #9)
GIRL, ESCAPED (Book #10)
GIRL, HIS (Book #11)
GIRL, LURED (Book #12)
GIRL, MISSING (Book #13)
GIRL, UNKNOWN (Book #14)

LAURA FROST FBI SUSPENSE THRILLER
ALREADY GONE (Book #1)
ALREADY SEEN (Book #2)
ALREADY TRAPPED (Book #3)
ALREADY MISSING (Book #4)
ALREADY DEAD (Book #5)
ALREADY TAKEN (Book #6)
ALREADY CHOSEN (Book #7)
ALREADY LOST (Book #8)
ALREADY HIS (Book #9)
ALREADY LURED (Book #10)
ALREADY COLD (Book #11)

EUROPEAN VOYAGE COZY MYSTERY SERIES
MURDER (AND BAKLAVA) (Book #1)
DEATH (AND APPLE STRUDEL) (Book #2)
CRIME (AND LAGER) (Book #3)
MISFORTUNE (AND GOUDA) (Book #4)
CALAMITY (AND A DANISH) (Book #5)
MAYHEM (AND HERRING) (Book #6)

ADELE SHARP MYSTERY SERIES
LEFT TO DIE (Book #1)
LEFT TO RUN (Book #2)
LEFT TO HIDE (Book #3)
LEFT TO KILL (Book #4)
LEFT TO MURDER (Book #5)
LEFT TO ENVY (Book #6)
LEFT TO LAPSE (Book #7)
LEFT TO VANISH (Book #8)
LEFT TO HUNT (Book #9)
LEFT TO FEAR (Book #10)
LEFT TO PREY (Book #11)
LEFT TO LURE (Book #12)
LEFT TO CRAVE (Book #13)
LEFT TO LOATHE (Book #14)
LEFT TO HARM (Book #15)
LEFT TO RUIN (Book #16)

THE AU PAIR SERIES
ALMOST GONE (Book#1)
ALMOST LOST (Book #2)
ALMOST DEAD (Book #3)

ZOE PRIME MYSTERY SERIES
FACE OF DEATH (Book#1)
FACE OF MURDER (Book #2)
FACE OF FEAR (Book #3)
FACE OF MADNESS (Book #4)
FACE OF FURY (Book #5)
FACE OF DARKNESS (Book #6)

A JESSIE HUNT PSYCHOLOGICAL SUSPENSE SERIES
THE PERFECT WIFE (Book #1)
THE PERFECT BLOCK (Book #2)
THE PERFECT HOUSE (Book #3)
THE PERFECT SMILE (Book #4)
THE PERFECT LIE (Book #5)
THE PERFECT LOOK (Book #6)
THE PERFECT AFFAIR (Book #7)
THE PERFECT ALIBI (Book #8)

THE PERFECT NEIGHBOR (Book #9)
THE PERFECT DISGUISE (Book #10)
THE PERFECT SECRET (Book #11)
THE PERFECT FAÇADE (Book #12)
THE PERFECT IMPRESSION (Book #13)
THE PERFECT DECEIT (Book #14)
THE PERFECT MISTRESS (Book #15)
THE PERFECT IMAGE (Book #16)
THE PERFECT VEIL (Book #17)
THE PERFECT INDISCRETION (Book #18)
THE PERFECT RUMOR (Book #19)
THE PERFECT COUPLE (Book #20)
THE PERFECT MURDER (Book #21)
THE PERFECT HUSBAND (Book #22)
THE PERFECT SCANDAL (Book #23)
THE PERFECT MASK (Book #24)
THE PERFECT RUSE (Book #25)
THE PERFECT VENEER (Book #26)

CHLOE FINE PSYCHOLOGICAL SUSPENSE SERIES
NEXT DOOR (Book #1)
A NEIGHBOR'S LIE (Book #2)
CUL DE SAC (Book #3)
SILENT NEIGHBOR (Book #4)
HOMECOMING (Book #5)
TINTED WINDOWS (Book #6)

KATE WISE MYSTERY SERIES
IF SHE KNEW (Book #1)
IF SHE SAW (Book #2)
IF SHE RAN (Book #3)
IF SHE HID (Book #4)
IF SHE FLED (Book #5)
IF SHE FEARED (Book #6)
IF SHE HEARD (Book #7)

THE MAKING OF RILEY PAIGE SERIES
WATCHING (Book #1)
WAITING (Book #2)
LURING (Book #3)
TAKING (Book #4)

CAUSE TO HIDE (Book #3)
CAUSE TO FEAR (Book #4)
CAUSE TO SAVE (Book #5)
CAUSE TO DREAD (Book #6)

KERI LOCKE MYSTERY SERIES
A TRACE OF DEATH (Book #1)
A TRACE OF MURDER (Book #2)
A TRACE OF VICE (Book #3)
A TRACE OF CRIME (Book #4)
A TRACE OF HOPE (Book #5)

CHAPTER ONE

Bobby Wayne was really worried that within two months' time, his family would be starving. Even though he had a job, it gave him no security. He'd been working for a cab company in Midtown Manhattan for about a year now and, for a while, things had been going great. Automobiles seemed to be an accepted part of life now, so the hesitancy to rely on them was quickly fading away. People had been generous in their tips and his stellar performance behind the wheel had even nudged his supervisors into increasing his wages a bit.

But then the market crashed. There had been rumors of it for a while but when it had actually hit, it was almost as if things had changed overnight. Many people no longer had the finances to be able to afford the services of a cab. And those that did were certainly not as generous with their tips anymore. In fact, the company he worked for had already released three drivers because of cutbacks and he was all but certain he would be next. He'd only had nine fares in the past two days, a time period in which he'd averaged about twenty-five previously.

Bobby knew if he lost his job, the savings he'd accumulated would get them through a few weeks. But if things didn't turn around soon, he was going to have to start planning for his family in a totally different way. He already knew that there were people starving on the streets—most of them immigrants, but people were people as far as he was concerned—and the thought of his family soon being among them broke his heart. He had three kids and a saint of a wife; the idea of not being able to provide for them and keep them comfortable gnawed at his heart.

Bobby was taking his cab around his assigned area for the sixth time, winding his shift down as he passed along the night-shrouded streets. There were people coming and going, a small hustle-and-bustle that New York City was coming to adapt as part of its charm, but there was a bit less joy and enthusiasm to it these days. Bobby thought even the rich and supposedly unbreakable were starting to feel the pinch of the market crash but were unable to admit it to themselves just yet.

But when they had to face it head on in several weeks or months, this city might look very different indeed.

The sad truth of the matter was that desperation was starting to sink in for a lot of people. Bobby could see that on the streets. The night crowds were getting thinner and, during the day, there seemed to be an invisible sort of weight pressing down on everyone. Here they were, in a city that kept creating buildings that seemed to want to burst the sky open, but now that very same sky was pretty much collapsing on their heads.

Bobby came to a stop at an intersection. He looked ahead and saw a street with just a few milling people, most of the lights already out at just ten o'clock at night. A month ago, it would have been a very different picture indeed. He just couldn't get over how quickly things had changed, how fast the city had brought so many people to a sudden halt.

He was so saddened by the sight of the streets ahead that he had no warning at all when the terrible, deafening sound erupted beside his cab.

He heard a slamming noise, something like metal being torn apart, and then glass breaking. It was so loud and sudden that Bobby let out a little shriek, jumping in his seat. He looked to his right and though he clearly knew what he was looking at, it took his mind a moment to process it.

There was a body stretched out on the hood of a car. Judging from the sound that had startled him, the wrecked condition of the hood and the shattered windshield, Bobby knew exactly what had happened.

This poor man had just jumped to his death. It was nothing new, not really. Bobby had read plenty of stories in the papers about people— particularly banker and investment types that had lost tons of money as a result of the crash-- jumping to their deaths or putting bullets in their own heads.

Bobby got out of his cab on shaky feet and started walking toward the tragic sight. But he made it no farther than the hood of his own car. It was just too awful. The man's neck had snapped, his left leg was bent at an impossible angle, and his entire body was twisted in a way that defied explanation. Bobby was grateful that the dead man's head wasn't turned in his direction.

And then there was all the blood. It was everywhere, visible even in the darkness and somehow sparkling in the shattered glass.

It was too much for Bobby. It wasn't just the brutal death of this man but, as he stood there on the darkened street, Bobby saw this man as the state of the city. And if things didn't change soon, he feared there

would be no hope for his family—or the millions of others that called
New York home.

CHAPTER TWO

When Ava had first started working under Captain Minard's watchful eye, she'd found herself nervous and on edge whenever she spoke with him. It had been even worse whenever she'd had to enter his office. The uneasy feeling had lightened up a bit when she'd become a detective, but she still felt a little out of place.

She felt that again as she looked at his office door. It was 12:56, and she had a meeting scheduled for 1:00. When she'd discovered Frank had also been called to join the meeting, she felt a bit better, but not much.

They sat together at Frank's desk, looking in that direction and waiting for the next four minutes to pass. Sitting in her anxiousness, Ava thought back over their last few months together—particularly how they'd quickly evolved from head-butting partners to something much more romantic. They were not lovers, because they'd not yet slept together, but the physical act was the only thing missing from the label. As such, she could usually read Frank fairly well but, right now, she couldn't tell if he was nervous or not; the man wore his expressions like a cheap, gray suit. It was impossible to read him most of the time.

"Do you have *any* idea what this might be about?" Ava asked.

"No. No more than you do. It could be about maybe dividing a few detectives up to create some sort of task force regarding the crimes and deaths related to this market crash. It's getting out of hand. There were two more last night. Did you hear about them?"

"Yeah." She *had* heard about them, but she tried not to obsess over them. She hated the idea that power and money had so much sway over how people viewed their lives. Money could be earned back, after all. A wasted life ended too early could not.

She also didn't think this would be the reason behind the meeting. She knew that Minard valued Frank's position as detective on his force. She highly doubted Minard would use Frank on some sort of side project to look into crashed market-based crimes.

Frank looked at his watch and lightly nudged her. He was trying to be playful, but she could tell he was also uneasy. In a strange way, it actually helped to calm her nerves a bit. "Might as well get to it, then," he said.

She let him get a few steps ahead of her, always aware of what they might look like to the other officers and detectives. When he was nearly at Minard's office door, Ava got up and followed after him. She watched as Frank knocked, waited for an answer, and then opened it. He held the door for her, and she also stepped inside. When she did, she noticed right away that Captain Minard was not alone.

The other man in the office was sitting in one of the chairs on the other side of Minard's desk—the side she and Frank typically sat on. He stood up when she entered and offered his hand to both of them. This was a huge show of respect as far as Ava was concerned, as most men would never think of extending such a gesture to a woman. She shook his hand as he smiled at her and though she had no idea who he was, Captain Minard filled her in.

"Detectives Wimbly and Gold, this is Chief Adam Freemantle," he said. "He's one of four chiefs that oversee all the precincts in the city."

"It's a pleasure to meet you both," Freemantle said. He looked to be a bit older than Minard and carried himself well. The shape of his shoulders made her think of her own father, who had been involved in boxing since the age of sixteen. Freemantle was completely bald, but wore a moustache that was perfectly trimmed.

"Same to you, sir," Ava said. Still, the presence of one of the primary chiefs at this meeting tripled her anxiety.

"It's an honor, sir," Frank said.

Freemantle didn't sit back down, but rather made sure to offer his seat to Ava. She took it with a smile, waiting to see why he was here.

"Detectives," Minard said, "Chief Freemantle is here because of an issue that has come to my attention in the last few days. I reached out to him and he was concerned as well. He wanted to be a part of the conversation we're about to have."

"Okay…" Frank said. "Is everything okay?"

Minard eyed them both apologetically and then leaned back in his seat with a forlorn look on his face. "Detective Wimbly, how long have you and Detective Gold been romantically involved?"

And there it was. Ava felt her heart skip a beat as a flush of warmth spread through her. She wasn't sure if it was embarrassment or fear (or maybe a bit of both) but she found herself unable to properly respond. It was a good thing Minard had asked Frank for a response instead of her.

"Not long," Frank said. She was impressed with how Frank didn't skip a beat or even waste a single moment trying to decide if he should lie or not. She was glad he had opted for the truth. The presence of Chief Freemantle made this a much more serious situation.

"Can you please be more specific?" Minard asked with a hint of irritation.

"Officially, maybe three or four weeks," Frank said. He looked to Ava and shrugged. "Is that what you'd say?"

She honestly had no idea, but she was fine going along with that answer. "Yes, I'd say that's fairly accurate."

"I'm sorry, sir," Frank said. "But is there a rule against it?"

"Well, that's why I'm here," Chief Freemantle said. "Because women in the precincts are such a rarity, there *is* no rule. However, we need to tread carefully here, as Detective Gold is something of a celebrity."

"A celebrity?" Ava asked, baffled by the word.

"More or less, yes. And don't get me wrong…I'm a huge admirer. Your track record and the way you have carried yourself has been great for the public view of the force. I do understand that some lines have been crossed here and there but that only adds to it. And as long as no one gets hurt, I'm willing to brush all of that under the rug. But a romantic relationship with your partner is a different matter completely."

"So…are we in some sort of trouble?" Ava asked.

"Oh, no, not at all," Freemantle said. "I believe Captain Minard and I have come up with a solution that works for everyone: both of you, the other officers here at your precinct, maybe even the force as a whole."

Ava watched as Minard and Freemantle shared a look, perhaps trying to figure out which one of them would be the one to present the solution. In the end, it was Minard—probably the right call as far as Ava was concerned, since he knew both of them relatively well.

"Because only a handful of officers have noticed and come to me with it, I believe we can keep it mostly quiet. But this also presents us with an opportunity. Chief Freemantle and I have decided that we are temporarily going to split you up. Detective Wimbly will stay here and resume his daily duties. Detective Gold, we'd like you to transfer to the Seventeenth Precinct. They are in the midst of something of a morale boost with a few new, promising rookies and we believe your presence there would really kick it into overdrive. In that area, such a boost is going to be very rewarding, given the current state of financial ruin. It's really hit the city hard over there."

Ava digested this all, not quite sure how to react and respond. It was flattering, sure, but the same move was also separating her from Frank. Romantic feelings aside, he'd been the only thing she'd known as a partner since the beginning. She'd come a very long way, mostly because of his support. She had no idea how she might get on without him by her side. Of course, she didn't want to say this and, more than that, the fighter in her welcomed the challenge.

"When would this begin?" Frank asked. She noted some concern in his voice and was surprised how much it touched her.

"Tomorrow," Chief Freemantle said. "Captain Minard and I have already gotten the paperwork ready. All we need are your signatures and we can get it started."

"You said this is temporary," Ava said. "How temporary? I only ask because I do live in the area, sir. And I have a son, as you know."

"Not too long at all," Freemantle said. "Four weeks…maybe six. And after that, we can step back and re-evaluate. How does that sound?"

She knew that she and Frank needed to take this. Both Minard and Freemantle were not only excited about this, but they both seemed to be very much on their side. She knew that Minard could have had a much different reaction to rumors of their relationship when they'd come to him. As far as she was concerned, this was an absolute best-case scenario.

"I think that's very fair," Frank said. Ava noted, though, that he seemed to find it hard to look in her direction.

"Me, too," Ava said. "Will I be partnered with someone at the Seventeenth?"

"Yes," Freemantle said. "And I think I already know a good fit for you." He looked to Minard and then to Frank and Ava, as if to make sure no one had anything else to add. When everyone was quiet for several seconds, he gave a single clap of his hands and headed for the door. "I think this is going to work out for the best. Detective Gold, I'll make sure you're all set up and good to go when you arrive at the new precinct tomorrow. If you have any questions, just direction them to Captain Minard."

"Thank you, Chief," Minard said, as Freemantle left.

Minard then regarded them. He didn't seem as delighted as Freemantle, but he was smiling, at least. "You two okay with this?"

"Yes, sir," Ava said. And while the idea of been taken away from Frank sat oddly with her, she was also surprised to find that the prospect of starting somewhere new was actually rather exciting. The longer she had to process it all, the more she welcomed the challenge.

"I think it will work fine," Frank said. "Is there anything else?"

"No. You're both dismissed."

Ava opened her mouth to thank Captain Minard but was surprised with how quickly Frank left the office. She nodded quickly to Minard as she walked out after him. She caught up to him as he was halfway across the room, cutting behind the bullpen area to get back to his desk.

"Frank? Are you okay?"

"I'm fine," he said, not bothering to look at her. He didn't sit down at his desk. Instead, he grabbed his badge and the holster with his sidearm and slipped it on.

"Are you sure?" Ava said.

"Yes. I'm just going to head out and follow up on some leads for a few smaller cases I was reading up on this morning. Things that really haven't even been properly assigned yet."

"Oh, okay," she said, sensing something very off in his demeanor and the way he was talking to her. "Do you need some help?"

He finally glanced in her direction, but it was brief. "No, thanks. You should probably stay here and figure out what all needs to be done about your transfer, right?"

It wasn't an insult or even a direct dig at her, but it hurt all the same. And quite frankly, it made her a little mad. "Yeah, maybe so," she said.

Without another word, Frank headed for the lobby and the front door beyond. Ava watched him go and when she sat down in his chair, she replayed the meeting in her mind. She was pretty sure she hadn't said anything to set him off. She could only wonder if the meeting itself and its outcome had gotten to him. Maybe he feared their separation more than she did—and maybe he noticed it and felt hurt.

Whatever it was, Ava figured he was best left alone for the moment. And with him gone, she couldn't help but wonder what it might be like at another precinct—a precinct where no one knew her outside of a few newspaper headlines and beyond just being the widow of a well-decorated detective. And thinking those things, she started to understand why Frank might be so affected.

And if they didn't talk about it soon, it might be incredibly harmful to their relationship.

CHAPTER THREE

"You're sure this reassignment has nothing to do with your performance?" her father asked.

The question stung at first, but Ava knew what he meant. He knew that she was doing a spectacular job in her role as detective, but he also knew how lots of male policemen resented the idea of women being part of the force.

"I'm pretty sure, Dad. I think it's all going to be okay."

Ava shared the news with her father and Jeffrey over dinner. As she'd assumed, they both thought it was an exciting new opportunity. Jeffrey even seemed to think she was some sort of hero because, the way he saw it, everyone wanted to be working with his mother.

As they talked about what this could mean for her career, as well as the challenges of working at a precinct that was half an hour away, Ava did her best not to be sidetracked by the fact that Frank was not there with them. He didn't always join them for dinner, but it had become rather frequent—around two or three times a week. Neither Jeffrey nor her father seemed to think anything much of his absence, so it was left unspoken.

It wasn't until she walked Jeffrey to bed that Frank was even mentioned at all, in fact. And when Jeffrey brought it up, it reminded her just how sharp her son could be at times. He had an eye for emotional detail that most adults would envy.

"How does Mr. Frank feel about you going to another place to work?" Jeffrey asked as she tucked him into bed.

She had to be careful how much she revealed about the situation, not wanting to upset Jeffrey over something she didn't quite understand herself. "You know, we really haven't had a chance to talk about it. But I'm sure he's fine with it. I think he'd agree with you—that it's a great opportunity. And besides… Mr. Frank and I will still get to see each other. Just not at work for a while."

"Do you know when he'll be back over to see us?"

"I don't. But maybe tomorrow after I'm done with work, I can stop by where I work *now* and see him. I'll ask him then."

That seemed to ease Jeffrey's worries for the time being. They read a chapter out of one of his favorite books and then Ava returned to the kitchen where her father was washing the dishes.

"This whole relocation thing," he said. "Are you really okay with it?"

"I think I am. I was a little uncertain at first but the more I think about it and talk it out, I do think it could be good."

"Well, speaking as a completely biased father, I think it's a pretty huge move—to have the Chief of Police actually make sure to speak to you and hand-appoint you to a new location himself. I think there will only be good things to come out of this."

"Let's hope so," she said.

She pitched in and helped with the dishes, already feeling the urge to step out and head over to Frank's place. She didn't like the way things had gone before they parted ways at the end of the day, and she hadn't realized until speaking to Jeffrey that she really had no way of knowing for sure when she'd see him again. After all, she was reporting to a completely different precinct in the morning.

As her father started to get ready for bed, going through his nightly ritual of washing off in the tub and brushing his teeth, Ava sat on the couch and put her shoes back on.

"Hey, Dad?" she called out.

"Yeah?" he answered from the bathroom. He came out, wiping his mouth off with a hand towel. "Did you call me?"

"Yeah. I'm going to head over to Frank's place. I really would like to talk to him one more time before this transition starts."

Her dad nodded, and she thought she saw a flicker of worry in his eyes. If he *was* worried, he decided to keep quiet, though.

"Sounds like a good idea," he said. "You okay?"

She walked over to him and gave him a small hug. "Yeah, I'm good."

She left the apartment and opted not to hail a cab. She could walk to Frank's apartment in roughly twenty minutes, and she thought the walking might do her some good. She walked the familiar streets at night, enjoying the lively feeling of it all around her: the hum of traffic, the murmur of conversations, and the overall sense of being in the midst of such a large and thriving place that, even as it suffered from the recent financial crisis, still seemed to be vibrant.

It helped bolster the growing excitement about working in a new place. Yes, she was upset about being removed from Frank but the positive aspects of it were becoming harder and harder to overlook. And as she thought about the inner workings of the plan that Captain Minard and Chief Freemantle had put into place, she couldn't help but wonder if her father had been right. Maybe she'd been given the mantle of detective at first with no other reason than Minard hoping she'd crash and burn right away, sweeping her under the rug. But if that had been the case, that plan had backfired in spectacular fashion. Rather than mope and complain about it, maybe the NYPD had decided to use it to their advantage. Maybe they recognized that they could use her brief but mostly stellar track record to help bolster the image and motivation of other precincts.

She'd gotten so lost in her thoughts that she didn't realize she'd come to Frank's apartment building until she was standing at its steps. She went inside and walked to the second floor, to his very small and basic apartment. Because he'd thought it was so important to get to know her family, they'd only ever come to his place a handful of times. And even now, as she stepped toward his door and raised her hand to knock, she realized just how much she felt like it was a new, strange place.

She knocked and waited, but got no answer. When she knocked a second time, she leaned forward, nearly placing her ear to the door.

"Frank?" she called.

She could hear no signs of movement from inside. She wondered if he had stayed behind at the precinct burning the midnight oil as it were, as a way to keep his mind off of what would be taking place tomorrow. He had clearly taken the news harder than she had but had opted not to say anything. She'd sensed this at work but had known better than to try to pull it out of him.

Feeling silly and a little defeated, Ava knocked one more time. When she still didn't get a response, she considered going to the station to look for him. But by the time she got to the front door, she rejected the idea. Even if he *was* there, he wouldn't risk speaking about something so emotional and personal at the office, in front of other officers.

She was just going to have to let it go for now.

She stepped back out into the night and looked in the direction of her own apartment. But as she did, she reached into the pocket of her jacket and fingered the small object she'd been keeping inside the pocket since yesterday. It was a book of matches with the simple logo of a place called the Ash Lodge. She'd taken it from the building where she'd nearly managed to apprehend the man that had killed her husband—a slippery little goon by the name of Jim Spurlock.

The night was wide open before her and if she chose to do so, she could look into this place. She'd yet to check in records and research at the precinct, knowing that it would send her down a deep, dark rabbit hole. And she'd been *far* too concerned about the meeting with Minard to give it much thought.

But now…if she wanted to, she could find this place and figure out how it was connected to Spurlock. She assumed it was just one of his little haunts, somewhere he fooled around with his fellow criminals. Then again, she doubted such an establishment would go and give away their name by placing it on the covers of their matchbooks.

She decided to just go back home. There was too much at stake, too much going on tomorrow. The last thing she needed was to stay out late chasing down leads that may, for now, be nothing more than phantoms. She retraced her steps, heading back home, wondering what Frank was up to right now…and wondering if her relocation might serve as the beginning of the end for their whirlwind relationship.

****

Frank had been sitting on his lounge chair, flipping through some old case notes when someone knocked on his door. He was certain it was Ava. He couldn't remember the last time anyone other than Ava had knocked on his door. His first instinct was to answer it, but he thought better of it at the last moment.

He knew the conversation that they'd have, and he wasn't ready to delve into it yet. It wasn't just because he wanted to avoid the conflict, but because he honestly wasn't sure how he felt about it. He hadn't told her, but he'd been dealing with another unspoken issue even before Minard had tossed out the re-assignment news.

He'd been really struggling with how obsessive Ava had become over finding her husband's killer. At the heart of it, he thought he could understand the drive and determination. Someone had killed the man she loved, and her son's father. Hell, he even respected her for it. But the deeper she went into it, the more dangerous it became. Not only did he fear losing her, but he was also reminded each and every time she found a new lead or clue just how much she'd loved Clarence.

And quite frankly, he wasn't sure if he could contend with that. He wasn't sure if he *wanted* to contend with it.

He cringed when she knocked a second time. And when she called out his name, he set the folders and reports down on the small table by his chair. He stared at the door, almost calling back to her.

But he let out a shaky sigh and sat back in the seat. He didn't move again until he could hear her faint footfalls walking away from the door, further back down the hallway.

He'd loved and lost before, so he was used to heartbreak. He knew that if Ava went to another precinct and excelled, she'd take her passion for finding her husband's killer with her. And before too long, he'd simply be pushed out of her life. Maybe not on purpose—he didn't think she had a cruel bone in her body—but it was bound to happen.

He figured he'd be doing her something of a favor by simply stepping aside now, before they got too deep into their relationship. Selfishly, it was easier this way for him, too. He'd never been particularly good at goodbyes.

As Ava's footsteps faded into silence on the other side of his door, he was pretty sure he'd just avoided a very big and painful one.

CHAPTER FOUR

Ava opened the door to the Seventeenth Precinct having no idea what to expect. So when she found a station that was considerably smaller and not quite as frantic as the precinct she'd been calling home for the last four months or so, she found herself baffled. Taking her first few steps inside, several faces turned toward her. All of them were male, most of them were young, and all of them looked just as uncertain as she felt.

She did her best to advanced farther inside without seeming rude. The place was quaint in an almost authoritarian way. The entire left side of the building was comprised of what looked like a large lobby. The floors were made of hardwood, and a series of offices lined the wall. The remainder of the open-floored space was made up of several desks. Some of them were positioned end to end so that two officers were stationed at what looked like one, single large desk. Further off to the right was a wide, but small hallway with more rooms and offices.

Ava headed to the left, toward the larger officers. She assumed she'd need to speak with the captain in order to figure out where she needed to go. She seriously doubted the Seventeenth Precinct had its own Women's Division, so this should be interesting.

As she started looking at the doors along the wall, she noticed that most of them were open—a completely different approach to how things were done in the much busier headquarters she was accustomed to.

"Need some help?" a pleasant, chipper voice asked from behind her.

She turned around to see a young, dapper man in police blues. He was tall, clean-shaven, and looked slightly nervous to be speaking with her.

"I think I might," she said. "I'm looking for the captain. I don't even know his name, but I think he's probably expecting me."

"Gold, right?" the young officer said. "Ava Gold?"

"That's right." She wasn't sure how she felt about the fact that this man knew who she was.

"Don't look too surprised," he said with a smile. "Everyone knew you were coming today. It's been whispered all around the building."

"Is that a good thing or a bad thing?"

The officer smiled and offered her a shrug. "I don't know. I guess we'll find out." He then pointed to the second door furthest away from them. "Captain Miller's office is right there."

She opened her mouth to thank him, but he was already gone. She wondered if there was some sort of stigma around talking to her or if he was just uneasy speaking to women. Was she going to have to go through the whole sexism thing here, too?

Suddenly nervous, she approached the door the officer had pointed to and knocked. It, like the others along the wall, was partially open and the voice that answered was loud and unhindered.

"Come on in!"

Ave stepped into the room and found what appeared to be the exact opposite of Minard's office. It was bigger, for starters, and much tidier—including the man sitting behind the desk. Captain Miller looked to be in his sixties, but carried the age well. His completely bald head gleamed under the electric lights. A well-maintained moustache covered his upper lip and his eyes seemed to shine a bit as he studied her.

"Detective Ava Gold!" he exclaimed. He got up from his chair and walked over to her. Like Freemantle the day before, he seemed to make a very big production of shaking her hand. She supposed it might be his way of letting her know that he saw her as an equal, or close to it.

"Good to meet you, Captain Miller."

"Oh, likewise. I was quite excited when Chief Freemantle told me he was sending you over to us for a while."

"And I'm excited for the opportunity."

"Have a seat," he said, gesturing to one of the empty chairs on the opposite side of his desk. As she settled in, Miller continued talking with a bit of excitement in his tone. "I do have to admit," he said, "that I'd heard of your father long before I heard of you. I grew up with a bit of an obsession with boxing. Even had a few dummy matches. But it wasn't for me. But I do remember seeing your father, the fabled Roosevelt Gold, in several matches. I was there when he knocked out Sonny O'Toole in under thirty seconds."

"I'll be sure to let him know he has a fan," Ava said.

"Okay, so let me get past that," Miller said with a chuckle. "I won't waste your time, as I already have a case for you. I've got you set up with a desk out in the bullpen. There, you'll find the small bit of paperwork that you'll need to fill out and complete. Your partner, Officer Pawlowski, is already out there, waiting for your arrival. Pawlowski has the notes and details on the case, so I won't spout it out now and have you listen to it twice. I know what you're capable of, so I'm not going to shadow your every move. Does that sound okay with you?"

"That sounds perfect," she said. But really, this had been the opposite of what she'd expected. She'd thought there would be a lot of training and supervisory hoops to jump through in a new precinct before she saw any time on the street. "But just to make sure I'm understanding you perfectly, you want me to meet with my new partner and head out to work a case today?"

"That's right," Miller said. "As soon as you can. Before I send you out to Pawlowski, do you have any questions for me?"

"None that I can think of right now, sir."

"Well, if any do come up, my door is always open. And truly, detective Gold…I am so very excited to have you here."

"Thank you, sir. Now… Pawlowski, you said?"

"Yes. You two have the pair of desks all the way out on the far right side of the bullpen."

Ava left the office, a bit astounded that she had been given a desk in the central area of the building, right in the bullpen with all of male officers. There was apparently no hiding of the women in the basement at the Seventeenth Precinct. Maybe this was going to be a great change after all.

She made her way back across the lobby and to the bullpen. She gathered numerous stares as she went, but they were subtle—the sort that were quick and fleeting as people worked at things from their desks. None of them seemed judgmental, more like everyone just trying to get a peek at the new detective.

Ava kept an eye out for the desk all the way in the corner and when she finally spotted it, she slowed her march a bit. As she drew closer, she was very confused by what she saw. As Miller had said, she was indeed positioned with a partner, their two desks pushed front-to-front just like the other set-ups in the bullpen. But the desk across from hers was occupied by a woman.

As Ava drew closer, the woman looked up. She was strikingly pretty, her blonde hair drawn tight behind her head. She studied Ava for a moment with intense blue eyes and gave a nod that looked rather forced.

"Ava Gold right?" she asked.

"Yes…and, are you officer Pawlowski?"

"I am. And from the shocked look on your kisser, I can tell you weren't expecting a woman." Pawlowski smirked and added: "Sort of like getting a taste of it from the other side, right?"

"A bit, I suppose," Ava said. "I do apologize. Captain Miller said nothing about my partner being a woman."

"Is that going to be a problem?" There was a thick undertone of aggression beneath Pawlowski's tone. From what Ava could gather, her new partner had decided not to like her from the very start.

Ava answered by taking the chair behind her vacant desk. "Not at all," she said.

"Good, because I was told that we need to head out and start digging into this sorry excuse for a case." She slapped at the folders on her desk as she said this.

Torn between the few papers on her desk that needed to be signed and the notes on Pawlowski's desk, Ava chose the notes. "What do you mean it's a *sorry excuse* for a case?"

"I mean there's no case here at all." She offered the folder of case notes over to Ava with an irritated look on her face. "I doubt they did this to you—to the infamous Ava Gold—back where you come from, but here, they saddle me, the lone female officer, with the duck soup cases."

"Duck…duck soup?"

"Easy. Easy cases that Miller doesn't think is worth the time of the menfolk."

"I see," Ava said. As she opened the folder, she wondered if this was actually true or if it was just Pawlowski's bad mood speaking. As she started skimming through the scant details in the report, Pawlowski got to her feet and slid her jacket on. She also recited the details of the case as she knew them while Ava read.

"There have been more than a dozen suicides in the last two weeks over this stock market crash. Threaten to take money away and men lose their minds because…oh God, where will they get their power and influence now? But there was one from two nights ago that seems to maybe *not* have been a suicide. As you can see, this particular man seems to have jumped from Chrysler Building. And because of that building's unfinished and already mythical status, it's apparently much harder to imagine someone killing themselves there. That's the gist I'm getting from all of this, anyway."

Looking over the notes, that was pretty much the story Ava was pulling from it, as well. And it also made her think Pawlowski was right. It seemed like the sort of case that would be assigned to someone as nothing more than busy work.

Then why was Miller so happy to see me? she wondered. *Was it an act? Am I going to be saddled to nonsense jobs while I'm here as some sort of punishment? And, if so, punishment for what, exactly?*

"So, you ready to head out and waste our time on this case?" Pawlowski asked.

"Yeah, in a minute. I need to sign all of these papers."

Pawlowski nodded and started for the doors without even looking at her. "Sounds good. I'll meet you out front."

Ava was left alone at her desk, still catching the occasional stray glance from one of the other officers and assorted employees. There was no pen on her desk, so she grabbed a loose one off of Pawlowski's. She read quickly through all of the verbiage in the paperwork, signing her name where appropriate. It took less than five minutes and when she was done, she hurried out to meet up with Pawlowski.

She was standing on the stairs, studying the streets below. Ava was once again struck by how pretty she was, but there was also a subtle strength to her. She could see it in her shoulders and the way her back and neck were sturdy as she scanned the streets. Ava guessed her to be in her early thirties but wouldn't be surprised to find that she might be a bit younger.

"Good to go?" Pawlowski asked.

"Good to go."

Pawlowski waved her on as she started down the stairs. Following behind her, Ava could still feel that bit of hostility emanating from her new partner and it made her miss Frank very much.

CHAPTER FIVE

Ava stood in front of the unfinished Chrysler Building, craning her neck up and finding herself slightly in awe of it. Living in New York City, she was used to tall buildings, getting taller and taller every month it seemed thanks to the arrogance of man. But even though this one was unfinished, she could tell it was going to be something special. It was almost enough for her to look past the rumored "battle for the tallest building" that was taking place between men named William Van Allen and H. Craig Severance. She'd often heard of men comparing egos, even right down to the size of their manhood, and this, to Ava, seemed no different.

From what she could tell, the building was nearly finished—all seventy-five or so stories of it—and she didn't see how it would ever be topped. She wondered if their would-be suicide victim had felt similarly about it.

As they neared the doors—another of the features along the lower levels that seemed to be perfectly complete—Pawlowski turned to Ava and frowned.

"Let's not kid ourselves here," she said. "There are lots of people in the city that know of you, or have at least heard your name. You should take the lead on this. Plus, *detective* sounds so much more impressive than *officer.*"

"You sure?" Ava asked.

Pawlowski nodded and gestured for Ava to walk ahead of her. Ava did, and they passed through the front doors, only to be stopped almost immediately by a large, sweating construction foreman.

"What the blaze are you ladies doing in here?" he asked.

Ava rather enjoyed the look that came over his face when she showed her badge. "Detective Ava Gold, and Officer Pawlowski, with the NYPD. We're looking into the suicide that occurred here two nights ago. According to our records, it was up at the highest point."

The man smiled, even chuckled a bit. He stared at them both as if he were looking at two kids playing dress up. "Well, yeah, I was told the police might come, but…"

Ava hoped he'd continue with what he was about to say. She could sense that he had reservations about two women looking into it, and she wanted to see how Pawlowski would react.

He made a smart decision, though, and simply shrugged. "We'll, we've got small freight elevators working right now, but they'll only get you as high as the fortieth floor. After that, you'll have to take the stairs. And whatever you do, when you get up to the top, *do not* lean on any of those walls. They're firmly in place but they need to be reinforced. I wouldn't want your pretty brains all over the street."

Pawlowski let out one of the loudest sighs Ava had ever heard as she strode past him. "Thanks for the concern," she said sarcastically.

Ava caught up with Pawlowski as she made her way beyond the front entrance. On the first floor, things looked perfectly fine and polished, though there were still sheets and traps put up to keep the interior from getting dingy and dirty. They found the freight elevators all the way to the right, in flimsy-looking shafts that were clearly only temporary. When they reached them—there were four in all—a small group of construction workers eyed them as if they were lunch. One of them even whistled and nudged the man beside him.

"Curious," Pawlowski said in his direction. "Has that ever worked for you?"

This shut the man up. He looked angry at first but then decided to stay quiet while his friends pointed and snickered at him. Before things could escalate, Ava pulled out her badge and flashed it at them. "NYPD. Let's act like we've got at least some sort of manners, okay?"

All eyes turned away from them at that moment as the elevator took them up. It started with a buckling jolt and then a thunderous grinding sound filled the small wooden-based elevator. Ava felt the tremors of it in her bones as the pulleys and cables did their job, pulling them farther and farther away from the ground. She'd been in a few elevators before, but only to go up two or three floors. Going up as many as forty boggled her mind and she tried not to think about it as the motor continued to churn above their heads. She couldn't help but wonder how Frank would be reacting in that moment, racing up the side of this monstrous building.

She glanced back over to Pawlowski, trying to get a read on her. Pawlowski was looking down toward her feet, as if making sure she didn't have to look forward or ahead. She was clearly nervous but doing her very best not to let it show.

Finally, the elevator came to a gut-wrenching stop. The little box swayed a bit and Ava did not like the sense that her legs were still moving even as the elevator had come to a stop. She did her best to keep her calm as Pawlowski looked over to her.

Pawlowski lifted the little metal-slatted door and they stepped off onto the fortieth floor. It was featureless as of right now, nothing but steel beams, concrete, and sturdy walls. Doorways had been cut into the halls here and there, but the floor was featureless for the most part. They found the stairwell at the far end of the hallway and Ava was quite relieved when she saw that the walls there were also very close to their final stages. She didn't know if she'd be able to climb them if she could look to her right and see the city looming down below.

"I have to ask you, Gold," Pawlowski said as they climbed the stairs for the final thirty flights. "Are you really as good as they say you are?"

Ava wasn't sure how to answer that. "How good do they say I am?"

"Good enough for them to write about you in the papers. Good enough so that you've got precinct captains squabbling over you."

"Oh. Then…I honestly don't know."

"Is that modesty or ignorance?"

"Maybe a bit of both. Now let me ask you, Pawlowski. Do you have some sort of a problem with me?"

"Nope," she said. "Not yet. If you want the bare bones of it, I'm selfish. I liked being the only dame in my station. I feel like they brought you in because I wasn't enough."

"I'm sure that's not the case," Ava said.

Pawlowski had no response to this. They both remained quiet as they finished the grueling climb up flight after flight of stairs. Ava couldn't help but wonder if *this* was why she and Pawlowski had been tasked with this job. She had no idea how long it took them to get to the top. What she did know was that her legs were aching and even without seeing the open expanse of New York City sky all around them, she could *feel* the height. It seemed to weigh down on her, adding some extra pressure to her lungs.

When the stairs came to an end, Ava found herself standing on a reinforced wooden floor, made of sheets of thick boards and beams. It was not finished like the floors beneath them, and neither were the walls. As a matter of fact, the wall behind them was incomplete, offering that view of the sky she'd not yet seen. She could feel the wind whipping; while it was not nearly strong enough to knock her down, it was enough to make her feel like she had to push forward a bit more than she was used to.

Several workers were moving around as if they weren't bothered by it at all. As she watched, three men were hauling a small metal rod to the other side of the floor, toward the open space that looked out onto nothing more than sky.

"You ever done anything like this?" Ava asked Pawlowski.

"No. I stood out on a balcony in one of those Manhattan high rises a few months back. But this…this is too much. Let's make quick work of these and get the hell down."

It sounded like a good idea to Ava as she continued to study their surroundings. Because the more she looked around, the less complete this floor seemed. She saw open spaces with sky peeking through, blocked by nothing more than steel girders and the most basic foundation materials.

Still, at the same time, she felt drawn to the danger of it. She and Pawlowski walked over to the closest wall and peered out between the girders. It was horrifying and thrilling all at once. No more than six feet rested between her toes and open space. And standing so close to the edge, the wind seemed to be just a bit stronger at her back.

"I dare you to spit," Pawlowski joked.

Ava stepped back, her heart slamming in her chest. As she did, one of the workers came hurrying over with a shocked look on his face. He was coated in sweat and wore a hardhat that sat on his head in funny but handsome way.

"What in God's holy name are you two dumb Doras doing up here?" he howled.

"We're cops," Pawlowski said, brushing him off as if she did this sort of thing every day.

Ava found herself once again showing her badge. "We're here to look into the man that apparently flung himself from the floor two nights ago."

"Oh, that jackass?" the man in the hardhat said. "I tell you, you have to be some kind of maniac to even think about it. That's a *long* fall." He softened his demeanor a bit and eyed them with something like concern. "You ladies be careful, yeah? Is there anything we can do for you?"

"Would you mind answering some questions?" Ava asked.

"Yeah, sure. But let me get James over here, too. He's the crew supervisor." He turned and cupped his hands over his mouth. "Hey,

James! come on over here. These cop ladies have some questions about that moron that jumped."

Ava watched as a man looking at blueprints by a stack of lumber came slowly walking over. He didn't look as friendly as the first man, but he also made no attempt to hide the fact that he was quite taken by both of them. The smile he offered them as he approached was the sort that let Ava know he was accustomed to flirting with women and getting away with it. To thwart this and stop it before it began, Ava once again showed her ID.

"We're with the NYPD," she said. "We're trying to find out more information about the man that seemed to have leaped from this very floor two nights ago."

The man—James, presumably—chuckled. "Yeah, you and a bunch of other folks. I don't even know how he got up here. Those front doors are supposed to be locked after hours. And there's even a security guy downstairs most of the night, too."

"Do you have any idea if any of that might have been different two nights ago?"

"Not for sure, but I don't see why it would. I mean…you work for the cops. You know about all these men killing themselves lately. A place like this…you bet your gams it's going to be protected."

"Do you have any idea if that security guard might still be in the building?"

"He might be. He works some strange hours. Nine to nine or something like that. If you hurry back down, you might catch him."

"And what about you, sir?" Pawlowski asked. "Have you had any men sort of lose it while working up here? Anyone you think might want to throw themselves off under the stress of the job?"

"Not at all. There are some that know for sure they won't be able to handle the height. And even then, with the ones that do work way up here, I make sure they take breaks. If you're up here long enough, it *can* mess with your head. Besides…after I heard about the incident, I checked in with all of my men. Everyone was present and accounted for."

"This guard downstairs," Ava said. "Do you know his name?"

"They call him Dooley. I think it's his last name. I've never spoken to the man."

Knowing it was already after nine o' clock, Ava felt the need to hurry back downstairs. Her knees, on the other hand, were perfectly fine standing still for a moment. "Thanks for your help," she said, already turning back for the door. Her knees and calves seemed to seize up at the thought of what was coming.

As the women made their way back to the stairwell, Ava noticed Pawlowski looked back to the nearly finished walls. She shook her head softly and said: "Could you do it? Working up here, I mean."

"I don't think so. I think it takes a special sort to deal with the wind and the heights."

And in saying that, she thought the same might be true of a man that might kill himself from such a height. What sort of trouble might he have been going through to make such a plan? Or, on the other hand, what sort of maniac would have lured him up there only to throw him off?

CHAPTER SIX

Ava was relieved to find that it was at least a bit easier to walk back down the stairs. They did very little talking along the way in an effort to save their breath. The only conversation occurred somewhere around the forty-fifth floor. Pawlowski, now in the lead on the way down, said something Ava had already wondered about.

"The elevators…all these damned stairs…you'd *really* want to have to kill yourself to go through all of this. I mean, it would be easier to just put a bullet in your head or hang yourself, right?"

"That's a little morbid," Ava said, "but yes. I'd agree with that."

"I think by the time I got off of the elevator and then saw all these stairs, I'd turn around."

"Almost makes you think someone was trying to make a statement," Ava said. "Maybe someone trying to prove a point."

All Pawlowski said in response was "Hmm."

They finished their trek down the stairs and came to the elevator. Ava checked her watch and saw that it was 9:16. If this Dooley fellow was a creature of habit, he'd be long gone by now, if her brief conversation with the foreman up top had been accurate.

When they finally made it back to the ground floor and stepped out of the elevator, Ava relaxed, noticing that she'd been quite tense the entire time they'd made their trip up—even on the stairs. Her legs and knees felt lighter and she walked with a fluid ease that she'd never noticed before. *Maybe just the way normal people walk when they aren't accustomed to just having been way up in the sky,* she thought.

There was a different group of workers on the ground floor now, roughly a dozen or so all standing in a circle and speaking quite loudly. Ava couldn't tell if there was an argument or if they were just trying to speak over one another. As she looked over, she noticed that one of them was the same man that had stopped them when they'd come in the front doors. When he saw her looking in his direction, Ava waved him over. He muttered something to the man beside him and then hurried over.

"On your way out?" he asked them.

"Well, we were hoping the night watchman might still be around. Dooley, according to one of the men upstairs."

"You're in luck! Dooley usually dips out around nine, but one of the construction foremen offered him some scratch if he helped clean up some of the mess out back. He's still out there if you need to talk to him."

"Out back?" Pawlowski asked.

"Yeah, just head out the front and go around the left side. You'll see a small space with a lot of discarded building materials. Dooley and a few others are out there right now."

Ava and Pawlowski thanked him and took his directions When Ava was outside, she found herself glancing up to the top of the building, in awe of the fact that she couldn't actually *see* the top when she was standing so close to the building. Her stomach rolled a bit when she thought of how she'd been way up there only moments ago.

They came to the side of the building, finding the clean-up areas easily enough. It was blocked off from the rest of the street by flimsy metal fencing, broken only by a single gate along the side to allow people in and out. There were five men working hard to carry scattered junk and debris into a series of large, black garbage containers.

"Excuse me," Ava said. "Is one of you named Dooley?"

All five of them turned around. Two stared with the eyes of curious adolescent boys, while the others looked concerned to have two young women at a worksite like this one. But of the five, one raised his hands rather bashfully. He looked to be in his late forties and in need of a shave.

"That's me," he said with an uncertain smile. "I'm Dooley."

This time, it was Pawlowski that flashed her badge. "NYPD. Can we talk to you about some of your duties in the building?"

Dooley looked confused now, his eyes narrowing in on the badge. "Cops? Is something wrong?"

"No, sir," Pawlowski said. "We just want to ask you some questions about some things."

Dooley nodded and stepped forward, coming through the gate. "There's not much to tell, though. I mean, the building isn't even open for operation yet. Won't be much longer though. They think maybe another three or four months."

"Do you work as the night security every day?" Ava asked.

"Nah. It's me and one other guy that sort of rotate."

"Were you here two nights ago?" Pawlowski asked.

"I was. Been here for the last four nights. The new guy will come on tonight and cover the next three."

"I assume you know about the man that seems to have jumped from the top two nights ago, correct?" Ava asked.

"Yes, for sure. But, you know, the first cops on the scene poked around, asking questions. And I'll tell you exactly what I told them: I never saw anyone come in. And I sit right there in that lobby all night. The most I ever get are some curious gawkers, coming by hoping to get a peek before the place opens up. But I haven't had a single person try to actually come inside for a few weeks now."

"Well, we know someone *did* come in two nights ago," Pawlowski said.

"Seems that way. It could have been while I was using the restroom. And there was a period of about ten or fifteen minutes when I did fall asleep."

"Is that common?" Ava asked. "Do you doze off often?"

"No," he said, suddenly seeming to regret that he'd said anything at all. "I mean…I could lose my job if people found out. I mean…no one has to know, right? I can't afford to lose this job."

The desperation in his voice was genuine and Ava couldn't help but feel a little sorry for him. "Okay, then," she said. "Between just the three of us, how much time were you…*unavailable* two nights ago?"

His sudden look of discomfort told Ava that he was starting to understand that he'd made a mistake. He'd openly invited such questions because he'd seen them as innocent, albeit curious, women rather than investigating cops. Therefore, he sounded almost ashamed when he answered: "Maybe an hour."

"Any clue what time?" Pawlowski asked. She made no attempt to hide her annoyance.

Dooley thought about it for a few seconds, but eventually shook his head. "No, I wouldn't know for sure. All I could tell you is that it would have been sometime after midnight."

"And during the time you were *actually* awake, did you see anyone wandering around out front?" Pawlowski asked.

"No. Nobody."

Pawlowski sighed, shook her head, and turned away. Ava was taken aback at the almost unprofessional manner in which the woman carried herself, but she also understood it. She'd felt equally frustrated with people while on a case, but she'd always managed to swallow down her true feelings and present a professional face.

"Thank you for your time," Ava said.

Dooley nodded and seemed to be very happy that was where the line of questioning came to an end. He went back behind the fence to continue his work as Ava hurried to catch up with Officer Pawlowski.

"That was a little rude, wasn't it?" Ava said as she caught up with her partner.

"Was it? I just didn't see the point in questioning a man that proved within the first few seconds that he has no problem lying—also a man that doesn't do his job well."

Ava agreed, but maybe not quite as angrily. She then realized that they had left the scene of the crime, as well as the only possible source for information. And here she was, playing catch-up with a cop that seemed not to care all that much about her job.

"So then what's your next step?" Ava asked. "Leaving potential leads behind so quickly, what do you think we should do next?"

"Get more information on him other than 'he may have committed suicide.' We have his name in the records. I say we dive deep down into who he was and see what answers we find there."

"No one has done that yet?" Ava asked, surprised.

"Not to my knowledge. After all...most everyone involved in this was more concerned about the potential black mark against the building. No one really seemed to care much about the man himself."

It was sound logic, so Ava didn't argue. She was still trying to figure out Pawlowski and figured a confrontation this early in their partnership would spell disaster. And because Ava knew lots of eyes would be on her, she was going to do her very best to stay in line. With that thought in her head she turned back to watch the Chrysler Building as it grew slightly smaller as they walked away from it, realizing that this case was going to be more than just solving a potential murder— but making sure she represented herself well in a new precinct, with a new partner.

CHAPTER SEVEN

Some of the officers had cleared out of the precinct by the time Ava and Pawlowski returned. Still, Ava noticed a few quick glares pointed in their direction as they headed back to their desks.

"You need some coffee?" Pawlowski asked.

"That would be great, actually," Ava said.

"One second." She then slid the case notes over to Ava's desk and said: "Help yourself."

As Pawlowski stalked away to what Ava assumed was the break room, Ava started to look over the notes again. She did much more than skim them this time. Now that she'd seen the place where the man had allegedly jumped from, she felt she had a better lens to view the details through.

The victim's name was Alfred Perkins, a detail that was not provided to the public until about five hours after the body was discovered because it had been in such terrible shape. It was sad that it came as no surprise to Ava when she saw that he had worked as an investor at a bank over on Wall Street. Ava noted the address as 40 Wall Street—an address that stuck out in her mind because she'd read in the headlines just three or four days ago that many investors and financial-types working at that address had lost monstrous amounts of money in the crash. Putting two-and-two together, Ava thought it was a logical assumption to assume that Alfred Perkins had been among them.

She made a mental note to try to find that article because she knew that there were several banks and firms that were in hot water; they'd lost not only their own money, but the money of many clients as well. It was an interesting dichotomy because it opened the door to two possibilities: first, that the loss of all that money could have easily driven Perkins to suicide; second, that he could have potentially lost the money of his clients, creating a list of people that might want to do him harm.

She had just gotten to the details of the very brief bit of information about the first officer on the case that had spoken to the wife when Pawlowski came back over with a two cups of coffee.

"Thoughts?" she asked.

"I think it looks like a perfect copy of so many other suicides as of late," Ava said. "Rich banker loses everything, and maybe even the money of his clients, and can't handle it."

"Any idea how long we'll be expected to work on this before Miller will take our word that it was a suicide?"

"I'm not sure it was," Ava said. "Not yet. If it had occurred at any other building, I might buy it. But I go back to there being some symbolism of some kind to this. Speaking of which…do you know where I could get a paper from a few days ago?"

"Back in archives," Pawlowski said. Then, with a smile, she added: "You're looking to see if he was one of those poor saps that lost the money of his clients, aren't you?"

"I am. Did you already look into it?"

"I did. And he was. I'm still waiting on one of the guys in Records to get back to me on it."

Ava sipped on her coffee and considered the best way to ask what was on her mind. "Would they not let you make those calls?"

"A dame? Calling a bank and asking about business practices and clients?" Pawlowski laughed out loud genuinely. "No way in hell!"

Ava wasn't sure what discouraged her more: the reality of what Pawlowski was saying, or her flippant attitude toward it. In that moment, something did click for her, though. She had to remind herself that not every woman in the city was as stubborn or as determined as she was. Some women, she supposed, were so used to being seen as second-class citizens that they had accepted it as their reality and used sarcasm or sour attitudes to cope. It seemed that Officer Pawlowski was a prime example of that.

"Okay, then," Ava said. "What about a visit to the wife?"

"Yeah, I think that needs to come next. As you can see, the first officer to speak to her did a pretty awful job."

Nodding, Ava closed up the folder and picked it up off of the desk. "Let's head back out then. Maybe we can get some new information out of her."

Pawlowski smiled and said, "You really are a go-getter, huh?"

"I'm just trying to do my job."

"Me, too," Pawlowski said. "it's just a little easier with a female partner that clearly isn't used to being told *no.*"

"What? You don't think I've been told *no* at work?" Ava was a bit surprised at the amount of anger that came out in the question.

Pawlowski seemed slightly cautious as she eyed Ava. Eventually, she shook her head and raised both hands softly in defeat. "Sorry. Wrong choice of words. Why don't we go ahead and try to speak with Mrs. Perkins?"

"Yes, let's."

Ava headed for the doors, surprised that Pawlowski was already getting under her skin. And here they were, less than three hours into their partnership. With the case file tucked under her arm, Ava continued for the doors, already feeling that this was going to be an impossibly long day.

* * *

Ava's first thought was that Stella Perkins seemed very relaxed and almost bored to have just lost her husband in such a grisly way. When they visited her home in a very nice house just a few blocks away from the hub of commerce where her husband had worked, she was sitting at her dining room table. She was drinking a cup of tea and speaking with a woman she introduced as her sister. Once it was discovered why the two female policemen were visiting, the sister recused herself to a different room.

Even after her sister was gone, Stella Perkins remained quiet for a while. She didn't even invite Ava or Pawlowski to sit down. She simply looked at her mug of tea with that same gaze of interest. Ava guessed her to be in her early thirties, pretty but in a plain sort of way. Her freckles and slightly reddened hair also made Ava think she might be of Irish descent.

"Let me guess," she finally said. "You two want to know if Alfred was the type that would take his own life. Is that right?"

"It is one of the questions I had in mind, yes," Ava said.

"Well, a week ago, I would have told you *no*. But the days leading up to Alfred's…death…he was not quite himself. It was to be expected, I suppose, given everything that was going on. But I had never seen him so worried and out of sorts. He wasn't sleeping and stayed sick to the stomach."

31

"Did he have any involvement with the Chrysler Building?" Pawlowski asked.

"None that I was aware of. Then again, Alfred knew many people. He may have known someone that was involved with the construction of it, or maybe had worked on a loan with one of the contractors. I'm ashamed to say I just don't know."

Ava found Stella's mood hard to grasp. She didn't seem sad but it was clear she'd been affected in some way. *Maybe,* Ava thought, *she's still processing it all.* She thought this was likely the case. After all, Ava knew better than anyone what it was like to lose a husband.

"Did he usually go out late at night?" Ava asked.

"Oh, no. I mean, there were nights when he wouldn't even get home from work until ten or so. But when Alfred was home, he was very much a homebody. And if he could, he would get into bed by nine and go to sleep."

"And what about the night of his death?" Pawlowski asked. "Had he already been home?"

"No. It was another of those late days."

"Had you already gone to bed?"

"I had. And then the next thing I know, there's someone knocking on my door. A cop, here to tell me that Alfred was dead. he told me what appeared to have happened and at first I didn't believe it. But then I thought of what he'd been like those last few days and really, it wasn't hard to believe. And…well, there's something else, too. Something else that makes me think he may have done it. I hate to think he took his own life, but I think…I think he may have prepared for it."

"What do you mean?" Ava asked.

"His life insurance. He had updated it several months ago, fortunately before all of this market crash foolishness occurred. The insurance company contacted me early this morning and asked me to come to their offices whenever I felt up to it. They told me how much money I'd be getting because of Alfred's death and it…I don't know. It made me think that with this market crash, he knew that if he *did* take his own way out, he'd at least be leaving us in a good spot financially even when he's lost so much money in the crash."

"You said *leaving us,*" Pawlowski said. "Who else is there?"

"We have a three-year-old son and a nine-year-old daughter. They're currently with my mother. My daughter is quite upset and whenever I would try to calm her, she just…well, she'd rather be with her grandmother. My mother insisted she take them…so I could take care of funeral arrangements, insurance things…"

"And I assume the children were here on the night we've been talking about."

"Yes, they were."

"No nannies or maids or anything?" Ava asked. As she asked, her heart seemed to stutter a bit. She realized in that moment just how methodical she was being. But she knew this woman's pain a little too well. She'd lost a husband recently, too, after all. It made her wonder what it might mean that she was able to compartmentalize this woman's situation and the case. She supposed it meant that the work she'd found as a detective—the very same job Clarence had enjoyed—had helped her to heal.

Stella frowned and took a sip of her coffee. "Well, we used to have a woman that served both functions. But we let her go two weeks ago because of the worries of money." She laughed softly, an almost forced noise. "And being a mother with no assistance these last few weeks…it's been eye-opening. But also lovely in its own way."

"Mrs. Perkins, have any of Mr. Perkins's co-workers or associates been by since it happened?" Aba asked.

"No. Not a single one. One of his partners did telephone me to give his condolences, but that's all." She sighed and showed the first sign of emotion since they'd arrived. "Ladies, I do appreciate the attention you're giving this, but I'm afraid your efforts are being wasted. As much as I would love to think that Alfred didn't do this awful thing…I believe it's exactly what *did* happen. I don't know why he chose that building other than…well, Alfred liked to do things big. I supposed he figured if he was going out in that way, he may as well make a spectacle of it."

Ava digested it all: insurance papers, kids at home with her, a sister that had been with her through most of it. These would leave trails of some kind, offering potential routes for her and Pawlowski to take. But in speaking with Stella, Ava was starting to think Pawlowski was right. All signs pointed to this being a suicide—that Alfred Perkins had pitched himself off into the sky from the top of the Chrysler Building, ending his life and troubles while providing for his family at the same time.

It was depressing, but also rather touching in a grim way. And oddly enough, Ava found herself hoping this was indeed what happened. It was certainly much preferable to the idea that someone had killed her husband in that same manner. But even as she and Pawlowski left, that possibility gnawed at the back of her mind, reminding her just how much work was involved in getting to the top of that building, of how desperate someone would truly have to be in order to go through with it.

"So where to next?" Pawlowski asked.

"I think we need to see where Perkins worked," Ava said. "I think it's time we take a trip over to Wall Street."

CHAPTER EIGHT

Ava found the building at 40 Wall Street nearly as intimidating as the Chrysler Building. Though she lived in the city and did her best to stay abreast of news and current events, she tended to ignore most of the stories coming out of Wall Street. This had become especially true since the crash, the suicides, and the infinite drama that now seemed to spill out of that part of the city. That's why she was surprised to see that the top portion of 40 Wall Street seemed to still be under construction. Apparently, though, the lower floors were fully operational.

When Ava and Pawlowski entered the building, they found themselves in a large, gleaming lobby. The floors were made of hardwood and, on the right-hand side, tile. The lobby led directly to one of the largest front counters Ava had ever seen. There was enough room for at least twenty people behind it, but currently there were only three women. One of them was chatting with a man in a suit and bowler hat. The one closest to them gave them a smile and waved them over.

"Good morning, ladies," she said. "Is there anything I can do for you today?"

Ava showed her ID and badge, something most women she spoke with seemed to be almost mesmerized by. This woman was no different, looking back and forth between the badge and the two women in front of her as if she were witnessing a bit of black magic or sorcery.

"We're Detective Gold and Officer Pawlowski with the NYPD. We're currently looking into the death of a man that worked here. Alfred Perkins."

The name registered with the woman at once. She frowned and nodded. "Oh my, isn't it just terrible?"

"Did you know him?" Pawlowski asked.

"Oh, not well. Just enough to wave and say hello as he came in."

"Would you happen to know where his office was located?"

"I believe he was on the fourth floor, though I don't know which office. Check in with Mr. White, on the fourth floor—he's the first office on your left. Mr. White was Mr. Perkins's supervisor. He can help you, I'm sure."

Ava and Pawlowski left the front desk and headed for the elevators. After their trip to the Chrysler Building, Ava nearly suggested they take the stairs instead, but kept it to herself. They took the elevator up to the fourth floor and as they entered the hallway, Ava was starkly reminded of how Wall Street was, in its own way, also feeling the crushing weight of the market crash. She saw empty offices and desks, cluttered boxes, and piles of papers that she assumed to be the belongings of workers that had either buckled under the pressure or had been let go.

It was almost eerie in a way, a detached sort of feeling that sank into her as they finally came to Mr. White's office. His door was open and when Pawlowski knocked, he looked up and gave them a huge, radiant smile.

He was a bear of a man, quite handsome in a rugged way. The suit he was wearing almost seemed odd fitting on him. He had the appearance of a man that might spend most of his time in the wilderness, not on Wall Street.

"Can I help you ladies?" he asked.

This time, it was Pawlowski that made introductions. White's face softened a bit, the huge smile fading at the edges when he learned why they were visiting.

"Well, his office is the fourth one down the hall on the left," White said. "You're welcome to have a look around if you like."

"Is there anything you may have noticed that seemed strange about Mr. Perkins in his final days?" Ava asked.

"Honestly, it's hard to say. There are so many men that work here that took hard hits when the market crashed. I had over a dozen men quit and a few that tried to stick it out but just couldn't recover. Alfred wasn't one of them, though." He chuckled here and then pointed up to the ceiling "Honestly, I think Alfred only stuck around to see how tall they could make this building."

"What do you mean?" Pawlowski asked.

"You gals haven't heard of the Race to the Sky?"

A bit of anger flared up in Ava. Even when they showed badges and it was known they worked for the NYPD, so many men still saw them as gals, broads, dames…whatever the current popular term might be. It was insulting but the sad part was that she didn't think most men were even aware of it.

"Just the basics. It's some competition between William Van Allen and H. Craig Severance, right?"

"That's right, exactly. There are three buildings here in the city and the owners are in this really immature but exciting little competition to see who can go the tallest. It's our building here, the Empire State Building, and the Chrysler Building."

"You're right," Pawlowski said. "That *does* sound very immature."

"And who is in the lead at the moment?" Ava asked, finding it hard to envision a building taller than the one she'd climbed earlier in the morning—though she did know that the Empire State Building might be very close.

"Sad to say, it's the Chrysler Building," White said. "The very same building Alfred used to…well, you know…" He cleared his throat and seemed to shift his emotions a bit. "That spire on top of the Chrysler Building was a surprise. No one knew it was going to go on there and then Walter Chrysler had the spire put up without even telling anyone. Damn thing pretty much went up overnight. And that put it in the lead by a large margin. It was something of a bet around here. Alfred was in on it, too. Sort of a running joke to see which building was going to hit God's feet first."

Ava had seen the spire he was talking about as they'd approached the building that morning but had forgotten all about it when she and Pawlowski had been standing on the unfinished floor, looking out to the sky. Just knowing that huge spire had already been attached to the structure before the very walls and supports of a few floors beneath it had been completed made her tremble a bit. All of that weight had been over their heads, and all of that open space had been out in front of them. It was dizzying to think about.

"Is Mr. Perkins's office unlocked?" she asked, wanting to wipe the thoughts out of her head.

"Should be. And as far as I know, nothing has been touched. I had someone get in touch with his wife and they let her know she was free to come when she wanted just in case she wanted to take some of the personal items. But if you need anything else, just let me know."

They left White's office, Ava latching on to one key detail she'd taken away from their conversation. She now knew that Alfred Perkins had at least some sort of interest in the Chrysler Building. If he was truly enamored with the so-called Race to the Sky, then the building would have been on his mind here and there throughout the day. That now meant that the Chrysler Building wasn't just a random location in his life.

They came to Perkins's office door and found it unlocked, just as White had said. Ava pushed the door open and found an office that showed signs of a busy, frantic worker. The desk that was located in the center of the room was littered with several piles of papers. A typewriter sat in the center, with a sheet of paper fed through. A ceramic coffee cup sat next to the typewriter, and there was a lightweight coat tossed over the back of the chair that was pushed under the desk.

The back wall of the office was mostly covered by old bookshelves that were stuffed with notebooks, papers, and folders. It was orderly, but a bit chaotic as well. As Ava studied all of this, she noticed the window along the back wall, nearly obstructed by the bookcase. She looked down to the street four stories below.

"You think that would kill someone?" she asked Pawlowski. "A fall from this height, I mean."

Pawlowski came over and looked down. "I think if it *didn't* kill you, it would cause enough problems to make you wish it had."

"He had a window right here. He had a four-story drop. So why hike all the way over to the Chrysler Building to kill yourself?"

"You heard White," Pawlowski said. "Perkins and a few guys were obsessed with these tall buildings. If Perkins wanted to go out in a big way, four stories just wouldn't cut it, right?"

"I guess not. Plus, his wife said he liked to do *big things*." She looked around the office again, wondering if she was doing something that Frank had often accused her off: making more of a case than was actually there. Of course, whenever she'd done it in the past, there had indeed been a bigger crime to be found. As such, she'd learned to trust her gut. And right now, her gut was telling her that there was a deeper story here—something more than just another devastated investor that had lost everything and then taken his own life.

Ava went to the desk and looked at the papers that were on top of their respective piles. She saw lots of numbers, little notes scrawled in ink, and terms she didn't understand. However, on a small pad close to the typewriter, she saw a list of names. There were six in all. She didn't feel that she needed to remove anything from the office just yet, so she grabbed a pen from Perkins's desk, found the nearest empty page on the pad, and copied the names down.

"Are you thinking those might be clients?" Pawlowski asked.

"Yes. And even if they aren't, they might be people that would be able to give us more details into what Perkins was like during his final days."

With the list copied down, she once again looked at all of those papers and binders stuffed into the bookshelf. She was sure there were stories of financial success in them, as well as tales of financial ruin. She couldn't help but wonder if someone with expertise in finance might be able to look through it all to give them a clear picture of how bad things had been for Alfred Perkins at the end of his life.

A clear picture was what she needed. So far, all of the small and scattered details made her feel uncertain. A fourth-floor office that had been left messy during his final day. A late-night trip to a building that wasn't yet complete. It was like looking at the cover of a book and deciding what it was about—a plain and simple suicide—but knowing there was more to the story in the pages that waited.

And to get the rest of that story, she'd have to go back to the original source.

CHAPTER NINE

"I want to go back to the Chrysler Building."

The comment was out of Ava's mouth before she was aware she was going to speak it out loud. They'd just left 40 Wall Street and were looking for a cab. She could tell just from Pawlowski's posture and ho-hum attitude that she was more than willing to call it a day and label the death of Alfred Perkins as a suicide.

"What in God's name for?" Pawlowski asked.

"To look the scene over with an eye toward the forensics side of things." When she watched Pawlowski roll her eyes, Ava added: "Are you telling me you actually paid close attention to the details of it all? That you weren't just a little hurried and scared because of where we were?"

Pawlowski shook her head at first, but Ava also saw her thinking, putting the pieces together. "Is this your way of showing off?"

"Showing off? How's that?"

"Making sure you analyze each and every inch of the case, making it seem like you're *that* dedicated to the job?"

"No, this is me *doing* my job—and feeling a little off my game because, honestly, we should have been looking the place over that closely from the start."

"Alfred Perkins killed himself," Pawlowski said. "It's a fairly simple case."

"Give me the rest of the day to look," Ava said.

"Oh, we can take as long as you want. I'd much rather be out on the streets looking into a case than sitting back at the precinct and pretending not to notice the other officers looking at me like I'm a steak."

Well, at least we have some *common ground,* Ava thought.

"I do have to ask you one thing before we go back over there, though," Pawlowski said.

"And what's that?"

She grinned slightly, the first true sign of happiness Ava had seen from her new partner. "You *do* remember all those stairs, right?"

Ava smiled back, but her legs already seemed to seize up a bit in protest.

＊＊＊

Remarkably, the climb back up the stairs the second time wasn't quite as bad. Ava found herself out of breath when they reached the top and her knees were aching, but that was about it. When they made it to the top, Ava made a point to find the supervisor they'd spoken with before. He was tinged with dust, sweating, and clearly irritated to be interrupted again but he took the time to speak with them.

"What can I do this time?" he asked. Behind him, a crew of seven men were working to stabilize a wall. Ava was again taken aback by the sheer bravery it must take to work so physically at such a height.

"It's a lot more than last time, that's for sure," Ava said. "But I'd like to give the entire open space a good look-over. And if at all possible, I'd like to ask that you and your crew not move around much."

"Are you serious?" he asked, inflecting some bass into his voice.

"I am. And if you cooperate, it won't take very long at all."

He looked back to his crew and then to Ava and Pawlowski. He removed his construction hat and glared at both of them. "Twenty minutes. That's all I'll give you. We've got a schedule we need to keep up with."

"Thank you," she said. His eagerness to keep working made her wonder just how stressed and rushed the construction companies on these taller buildings were in order to win the Race to the Sky.

She then looked over to the side of the building that Alfred Perkins had fallen from. It was partially built, with about a quarter of the wall missing, revealing the struts and metal foundations. She peered up and though her view was broken by a series of metal rods and temporary ceiling placements, she imagined the spire up there, pointing to the sky and standing firm to make the building the tallest in the city—for the time being.

"You're not great at making friends, are you?" Pawlowski asked as they slowly walked in that direction.

"I'm not interested in making friends," Ava said.

"Well, that sure explains a lot."

Ava had no idea if Pawlowski legitimately had something against her (other than the lame excuses she'd trotted out earlier) or if she just

41

enjoyed getting under people's skin—but the woman was about to get on her last nerve. To avoid losing her cool, Ava focused on the floor ahead of them…the floor, the beams, the rods, the rivets, and the vast expanse of open sky in front of them.

They approached the area slowly, coming to a stop less than two feet away from the open space within the wall. While there were two large metal beams running horizontally across to offer support to the walls that would eventually go up to close off this side of the building, it was still terrifying to even *think* about looking down.

"Well, here's one thing to consider," Pawlowski said as she inched slightly closer to the space where the floor ended and the open air began. "There's no way he jumped from here. If he did, he would have probably hit his head on one of those beams."

Ava noticed this, too. She didn't dare get any closer to the edge, but she did note that it wouldn't take much effort to get out onto one of those beams. She'd seen the pictures in the papers of the construction crews up in the air, balancing on these things as if it were nothing. In fact, if she were to take one more step along the floor and then one step out across that endless, open space, her foot would land on the beam rather easily.

After that, though, there was only her balance. One quick, sudden movement or a violent gust of wind, and she'd fall just as Alfred Perkins had. The two beams were about ten feet apart; one ran almost perfectly symmetrical to the floor while the other touched what would eventually serve as the ceiling.

As she looked to the lower one, she thought she saw something that stood out just a bit. The beam itself was a dark gray, so dark it was almost black. But almost directly ahead of her, there was a slight smudge along the base of it. The smudge was on the edge farthest away from them, so she couldn't see it for sure. The beam had a small layer of dust on it and the smudge seemed to break the layer apart a bit.

"Pawlowski? Look at the lower beam, on the side farthest away from us. Do you see that…almost directly in the center?"

Pawlowski inched forward just a bit more and then very slowly got down to her knees. Ava's heart froze in her chest as she watched. Pawlowski's knees were no more than a foot away from the edge. The wind whirled and countless building and ant-sized people waited down below.

"I do," Pawlowski finally said. "Could be nothing."

Oh God, Ava thought as she inched even closer. Her toes were now less than six inches from the edge and when she looked down, her stomach felt like it was doing a barrel roll. It was hard to focus on that one spot along the beam, but she managed to make herself do it.

Now that she was closer to it, the smudge became a bit more pronounced. She thought it might be a footprint, but if it *was,* it was pointed to the right rather than a partial print that was pointed *out.* In other words, it looked more like a footprint that was walking along the beam rather than one that had been positioned there to launch a body. The only issue there was the fact that there was only a single print.

The angle was all wrong for someone that had leaped to their death. Unless Perkins had decided to try his balancing act out before he took that leap.

"Did you see this?" Pawlowski asked.

Relieved to have a reason to look away from that yawning space, Ava turned and stepped further away from the edge. Pawlowski was looking down at the floor. There was a scuff mark along the unfinished concrete floor. In fact, there were two of them—both small and maybe part of the same one with a broken space along its center. Located roughly a foot away from it was a partial footprint—a boot, from the looks of it. This wasn't anything to write home about, as there were plenty of partial boot prints scattered around through the dust—but the others were a good distance away from the one near the scuff mark. It was also pointed directly toward the open space in front of them.

"Would you go get the supervisor?" Ava asked.

Pawlowski nodded and did as she was asked. There were no smart comments or objections this time, making Ava wonder if Pawlowski was finally starting to open her eyes to the fact that there might be more to this story than met the eye.

Ava looked back to the faint footprints she and Pawlowski had left in the dust, noticing that they were a bit more pronounced than the others. She looked over to the wall that the crew had been putting up when she and Pawlowski had arrived. She estimated it to be about seventy-five feet away, give or take a few feet. And there appeared to be several sections of wall that had recently been put up beyond it, going in the other direction. Of course, Ava was willing to admit that she knew nothing about construction and could be completely wrong.

Pawlowski came back with the supervisor. He seemed absolutely terrified that the two women were so close to the edge.

"What is it?" he asked, his voice thick with irritation. but then he apparently saw something concerning in Ava's expression because his tone changed when he asked: "Did you find something?"

"Maybe," Ava said. "These beams right out there…when was the last time anyone on your crew would have stepped out on them?"

"On those?" he asked, eyeing them. He took a moment to think about it and then shrugged. "I can't tell you for sure, but I know it's been *at least* a week."

"So certainly not in the past two or three days?"

"That's correct."

"And when did you have them start working this floor?"

"Seven or eight days, I suppose."

"Have there been many men over here, where we are right now?"

"I'm sure some have wandered around a bit here and there. But in terms of active work? No."

"What do you make of *that?*" Pawlowski asked, pointing out to the print on the beam.

He took a few steps forward, moving with the confidence of a man that had spent a lot of time up in these heights. When he leaned forward, his face out into the open air, Ava felt her stomach flutter again.

"It's definitely a print," he said. "But…there's only one. I don't see a second foot or even a trail of where the person went."

"Yeah, I noticed that as well," Ava said.

"And there's…wait. That's not one of my guys. I can tell for certain."

"How so?"

"All of my men wear boots. I make them…as part of just being safe. If you look at that print really closely…that looks like a flat foot. Like a dress shoe or something. You see it? Almost no tread on that thing."

Ava did notice it now that he pointed it out. When she compared it to the ghosts of prints all around her, the difference was quite clear.

"What about this one?" Ava asked, turning, and pointing to the recent-looking print near the scuff mark. As she looked at it, she noted that it did look similar to the others that were out closer to where the walls were actively being constructed.

"It's a boot," he said. "But it's impossible to tell if it's one of my guys or not."

"Is there any way you can keep your men from coming over here for a while? Maybe just like a day or so, until we can get someone up here to take a photograph of that print?"

"That shouldn't be a problem, so long as you can get it done in the next day or two."

Ava nodded and scanned the area, making sure they hadn't missed anything else. The partial print out on the beam was the most interesting, the clue that now had her more convinced than ever that there was something more to this story other than suicide.

"Anything else?" the supervisor asked.

"No, I don't think so," Ava said. "Thank you for your help."

"Of course."

"We'll be out of here soon," Ava said.

He took that as his dismissal and went back to join the rest of his crew out of sight. Ava and Pawlowski both looked back out to the beam, trying to put the pieces together.

"You really think the PD is going to send a photographer up here for these prints?" Pawlowski asked.

"Why wouldn't they?"

"Because I don't see the prevailing theory of suicide being changed because two women found part of a print. Sending more resources out here is only going to be further admission that there might be something other than a suicide."

It was a good point. But at the same time, Ava wondered what exactly had happened to Pawlowski during her time with the department to make her so jaded. What had made her so sure that she'd be disappointed and overlooked at every turn?

"And you know…that print out there might not prove anything. It could be from a week or two again and the definition has faded."

Again, a good point—but Ava was more inclined to go with the more pressing solution, the one that seemed to make the most sense.

"You really don't want this to turn out to be a homicide, do you?" Ava asked. "Are you that lazy, Pawlowski? Do you hate the job that much?"

Pawlowski glared at her, a blast of anger shining in her eyes. After locking eyes with Ava for a handful of seconds, she turned away and spoke back over her shoulder.

"We should get out of here," she said. "These men need to get back to work."

Ava almost argued further, but didn't see the point. Instead, she looked back out to that beam and the partial smudge on it. She imagined what it must be like to step out onto that beam at night as the city shone below you, the air and the lights and the sounds all calling you home.

She suppressed a shiver and then followed after Pawlowski.

CHAPTER TEN

When they returned back to the station, Pawlowski took it upon herself to go about her own business. She didn't speak to Ava a single time, even when they were sitting across from one another at their adjoined desks. Ava watched as Pawlowski busied herself with filing away paperwork and moving around the precinct in search of aimless things to do.

Ava didn't let this bother her. She understood the stress and expectations placed on a woman in this work environment. But what she didn't understand was why one woman officer would intentionally try to make it harder on another woman. Thinking it might just be a very strange territorial issue with Pawlowski, Ava ignored it. She had set her mind to proving that Alfred Perkins hadn't actually killed himself.

After putting in the request for a photographer to visit the site, Ava turned her attention to the list of names they'd found in Perkins's office. She walked back to the records department to run searches on the names and after an hour and fifteen minutes, came up with nothing. The closest she came was when she researched a man named Peter Smythe. He'd filed a complaint about a vagrant that had assaulted him on the way home from work two years ago. Other than that, the list of names netted nothing.

But she thought she knew someone who might be able to help her with the list. As the idea came to her, the desk across from her was still empty. She thought about hunting Pawlowski down, but the woman had already made it clear: her mind was made up on the matter. And if she was going to insist there was no case here, Ava didn't see the point in wasting her time trying to convince her otherwise until there was more proof.

So, without running the idea by Captain Miller or searching the building for Pawlowski, Ava left the precinct and caught a cab back to 40 Wall Street. She hated that a good portion of her day had been spent backtracking, visiting places she'd already visited, but sometimes a case felt like that—like creating a tight knot of loops rather than a steady line towards a definitive answer.

On the drive over, she couldn't help but wonder what Frank was up to. It hurt her to know that something was placing a wedge between them. The idea that she may not be able to share the day's events with him over dinner pained her. She'd love nothing more than to see the look in his eyes when she told him about being at the very top of the Chrysler Building, looking down through an unfinished wall.

She'd known he was bothered by her insistence of hunting down her husband's killer—a man she now knew to be Jim Spurlock. That alone had created some unspoken tension between them. She just couldn't help but wonder if this reassignment was going to be the final thing that did them in. She felt that they could make it work—that it may even make their relationship stronger—but she didn't see the point in fighting it if he had no interest.

Thoughts of Frank preoccupied her to the point of not even realizing she'd arrived at her destination until the cabbie brought the car to a stop. She paid her fare and stepped out in front of the 40 Wall Street building for the second time that day. She skipped by the front desk this time, making her way up to the fourth floor where she once again knocked on Mr. White's door.

"Detective Gold," he said with that same smile. "Back so soon?"

"Yes, I hope that's okay. I have a few more questions, based off of something I found in Mr. Perkins's office. Do you mind?"

"I'll see what I can do. What have you got?"

She took the list of names from the pocket of her jacket and handed it over to him. "I found these names on a pad in his office. I was wondering if you could tell me who they are. I assumed they might be clients of his."

White looked at the list for about two seconds before he started nodding. "That's exactly what this is. Looks like some of his more high-profile clients. In fact, this man right here, Stanley Umbridge, lost his entire life savings during the crash. He moved his family down to Virginia last week. Came in yelling and screaming but by the time the whole ordeal was over, he was crying into Alfred's arms."

"By any chance, would you be able to point me to some of the documents concerning these clients? I don't know if you're aware or not, but his office is sort of—"

"A mess, right?" White interrupted. "But damn if he didn't know where everything was. No matter what you asked him for, he would get it for you in under a minute. But as for these men…you should find everything you need in a binder that's inside his desk—a drawer right there at the bottom. It's a thick, black one. He showed it to me several times while we were discussing numbers as we smelled the crash coming along."

"Thanks so much," Ava said. She left the office and returned to the office further down the hall. Now that she knew what to look for, she ignored the stuffed mess of Perkins's bookshelf. She opened up the bottom drawer of his desk and found it in much better shape than the bookshelf. There were several folders and binders in the drawer, filed and organized neatly.

There were several black folders, but only one that fit the thick description White had given her. She removed it and found out at once that she had the right folder. Inside were several pages of documents attached to one another, the first page labeled with each client's name. Much of the work on the pages were hand-written, only a few here and there having been typed up. Just like the majority of papers on his desk, it was mostly numbers and terms that Ava wasn't familiar with.

She set it to the side, wondering how hard it would be to take the binder with her. Would White let her take it? Would Miller get upset that she'd made such a decision on her own? She still thought there might be some answers hiding in the numbers somewhere and hated to leave the binder behind.

She was about to shut the drawer when she saw a single sheet of paper, all by itself. It was sitting where the binder had been, making her assume it had fallen out. She reached in and took it, a plain sheet of white paper. It was slightly crumpled but the contents were still easy to read.

It was a letter, dated four months ago, from a man named George Albrecht. She read over it and managed to get the basic idea even though it was littered with industry jargon that went over her head. And when she thought she did understand what the letter was saying, she read it again just to be sure—because if she *was* reading it correctly, the implications could be enormous. One passage in particular caught her eye and, she thought, might be something of a smoking gun. That passage read:

As you know, investors change their minds on investments all of the time, often as frequently as every day or so. I do not believe anyone would so much as blink an eye if a few investors in your arena brought their money and attention over to a newer and more exciting investment like the construction of the Chrysler Building. Naturally, no one would have to know of your involvement. Even your employers would not be privy to any matters you and I discuss. Any money you stand to lose in sending investors to my team would be recouped once their business was firmly in place on my end.

From what she could tell, Albrecht was one of the developers at the Chrysler Building. Several times throughout the letter, he referred to "my team" as he went into detail about how he, Albrecht, wanted to work with Alfred Perkins to pull investors away from work and interest at the 40 Wall Street building and point them and their money over to the Chrysler Building. A closing note also suggested that this letter was not the first Albrecht had sent to Perkins.

She felt certain that taking the note, or the binder for that matter, would be crossing lines. Still, the letter was particularly damning, so she folded it and placed it into the inner pocket of her jacket. It showed a direct connection between competitors, and one that Perkins had clearly been trying to hide. Because the binder wouldn't be so easy to conceal, she placed it back into the drawer and left the office.

On her way out, she stopped by White's office one more time. This time when he responded to her knock she could see aggravation in his face. She didn't blame him, really. This was, after all, the third time she'd interrupted him today.

"I'm sorry," she said, not even bothering to walk in through the doorway. "I was just wondering what you know about a man named George Albrecht?"

"I don't know the man all that well, but I do know he's one of the primary developers over at the Chrysler Building. There's maybe a dozen or so men pushing the money around on that building and from what I hear, Albrecht is probably the most relatable. He's wealthy, but not in that way that makes him think he's better than anyone. Know what I mean? From what I hear, he's one of the few developers that actually shows up on-site to see how things are going."

"Have you ever worked with him at all?"

White chuckled and shook his head. "No, not me."

"And do you know if Mr. Perkins had any ties with him?"

White thought about it for a moment but shook his head at this, too. "If he did, I wasn't aware of it. And I honestly can't think of why Alfred would have had any reason to associate with him." He shrugged sadly and added: "Of course, it could be a friend-of-a-friend sort of situation. Do you mind if I ask why?"

She didn't want him to know that she'd taken the letter so she decided not to even mention it—especially considering the content of it. But she also didn't see the point of flat out lying. "I saw the name in some of his notes and thought it sounded familiar. I was just wondering. And with that, I'll leave you alone. Thanks again for all of your help."

She got back into the elevator and headed down to the main lobby. On her way out, she paused by the large front desk as a thought popped into her head. She approached the woman she'd spoken with earlier and tried on her very best smile.

"I need to make a call," she said. "Does this building still use party lines?"

"No, Detective," the woman said, sounding quite proud. "We've had access to direct-calling for about five months now. And of course, the people we call will also need to have direct calling for it to work. It still has its bugs here and there, but it seems to work fine most of the time. Can I make a call for you?"

She took the letter out of her pocket and looked at the letterhead it had been written on. *Fulton and Donner Enterprises.*

"Do you have Fulton and Donner Enterprises in your directory?"

"I believe we do," the receptionist said, pulling over a large journal-type book with several hand-written contact numbers. She scanned the pages for about thirty seconds and tapped it in delight. "Right here. I can make that call for you if you like."

"Yes, I'd appreciate that."

The receptionist used their new rotary phone to make the call. As Ava watched the wheel turn, the phone clicking the numbers home, she was astounded at just how quickly such an accomplishment had come to the city. Just five years ago, such a thing was incredibly rare. Now it seemed that there were direct-call rotary phones in most areas of the city.

Once the number was in, the receptionist leaned across the counter and handed Ava the phone. Within a few moments, she heard the surprisingly clear voice of another woman in her ear.

"You've reached Fulton and Donner Enterprises How may I help you?"

"My name is Ava Gold, a detective with the NYPD, Seventeenth Precinct. I was hoping to speak with Mr. George Albrecht."

"Oh, I'm sorry, ma'am, but Mr. Albrecht and several others are in a meeting right now. From what I gather, it's very important."

"I see. Any idea when he'll be out of it?"

"I'm sorry, but I don't know. I'd be happy to take a message and make sure he gets it."

Ava took a moment to consider her options. She wondered how much this woman might know about Albrecht and the so-called Race to the Sky. "You know, I think that's okay," Ava said. "I wonder, though...the questions I have are very basic. I wonder if you might be able to assist me. Do you work closely with Mr. Albrecht?"

"Not very closely, but I know enough about him, I suppose. I can try to answer any questions you have."

"Well, I understand that he's working very closely with some of the contractors over at the Chrysler Building. We're trying to get a read on what builders he's working with." She felt a lie coming on and was a bit ashamed of the ease at which it arrived. She was even more ashamed when she used it without much thought: "Bear in mind now, this isn't in pursuit of Mr. Albrecht himself. We're looking into some unscrupulous details and reports about one of the builders."

"Oh, I see," the woman said in a hushed tone. "Well, I'm afraid I don't know much about the contractors he's working with. Besides that, the details of all of their investments are kept pretty private."

"Oh, I'm sure. But I wonder if you might know the last time Mr. Albrecht visited the site?"

"I believe he's been over there at least once every day for the past week or so. Just last night...no, wait...two nights ago...he met with a few men over there after he left work. They treated him to a private tour of the building, seeing as how it's so close to being done."

"Two nights ago, you said?"

"Yes."

Two nights ago, she thought. *The night Alfred Perkins was killed.* Suddenly, the clandestine letter she'd found between Albrecht and Perkins seemed a bit more than just a thinly veiled attempt at funneling money and investors.

Just to keep up appearances and to make the lie seem more authentic, Ava added: "I don't suppose you know who arranged that tour, do you?"

"Sorry, I don't. Are you sure you don't want to leave a message?"

She considered it for a moment before declining and ending the call. She had the letter linking Albrecht and Perkins, and now knew that

Albrecht had been in the building on the same night Perkins had killed himself.

No, she did not want to leave a message. She didn't want George Albrecht to know she had called. She didn't want him to know she was coming.

CHAPTER ELEVEN

Ava grabbed lunch on her way over to the address she had for Fulton and Donner. It wasn't located in one of the three buildings that were part of the Race to the Sky, but it was still an impressive place. It was only three blocks away from 40 Wall Street, a smaller three-story building made of steel and glass. Just looking at it gave the impression that whoever worked inside had to be of some importance.

She ate her deli sandwich and drank her pop on a bench across the street, formulating a plan. She was well aware that Step One of the plan should probably be to go back to the precinct to fill in Pawlowski but she felt that would be a waste of time; there was traveling over to the station, trying to convince an uninterested party, and then traveling back. She figured this way, she was saving at least an hour and a half and sparing the aggravation of a new partner that was already getting on her nerves.

The busy thrum of Wall Street was unlike any other part of the city. Even in the midst of the market crash, it still seemed to possess a vitality that other areas in the growing city just couldn't match. Businessmen hurried along the streets, as if trying to escape the sad reality of the current financial situation. Vendors were still trying to peddle their wares here and there along the street corners. And above it all the buildings loomed high above them like sentinels.

Ava took it all in as she finished up her lunch. She honestly didn't have much of a plan when she crossed the street. If Albrecht was still in his meeting, she may have to pull her badge and get forceful, insisting that she speak with him. Also, she had the letter in her jacket pocket if she really needed to press the issue.

When she entered, she found the front lobby eerily similar to the one back at 40 Wall Street. It was a bit smaller and compact, but still spoke of power and influence, backing up the feeling the building gave from the outside. There was only one woman sitting at the desk up front, probably the same woman she'd spoken to on the phone. Ava approached her with a friendly smile, surprised at the bit of freedom she felt without a partner at her side.

"Hey, there," Ava said to the woman. "You may very well be the lady I spoke to on the phone about forty minutes ago. I'm Detective Ava Gold. I'd called with some questions about Mr. Albrecht."

"Yes, of course," the woman said, returning her smile. "And no more than ten minutes after you called, their meeting came to an end. As far as I know, Mr. Albrecht should be in his office."

"Oh, thank you so much. Where is that located?"

"Second floor, Room 28. But I should warn you…whatever was discussed in that meeting left most of the men that came out in sour moods." She sighed and leaned forward, as if about divulge a secret. "It's been this way pretty much every single day since the market crashed."

"I can't imagine how stressful this line of work must be during a time like this," Ava said. She gave a polite nod, gave her thanks, and then headed for the elevators. When she saw the group of men, bickering and arguing as they also waited, Ava opted for the stairway. She found the door to the stairs on the left side of the lobby and walked to the second floor.

Here, she found a stark difference between the Fulton and Donner offices and the offices at 40 Wall Street. Every door was closed and even without knocking on a single one, there was a tension she could feel in the air. It almost made her rethink her plan of just knocking on Albrecht's door to see what he'd be willing to openly offer her in the way of testimony. But she forged on, finding Room 28 and knocking on the door.

The verbal response she got was almost like a barking dog. She clearly heard the *"Yeah?"* from the other side but there was so much anger and irritation to it that it almost sounded like growling.

With her nerves on edge and ready for anything, she opened the door. She found a man smoking a pipe and furiously looking over a series of papers. He looked angry and tired, his graying hair in disarray. He barely even looked at Ava before responding.

"I said *yeah*," he said. "I did not say *come on in.*"

Ava nearly apologized for her intrusion; that's how unexpectedly hostile Albrecht was. Instead, she stepped inside and took out her badge. "I'm Detective Ava Gold with the NYPD," she said. "I'd like to ask you some questions."

"Not now," he barked. "As you can see, I'm busy as hell and I don't have time for questions."

"With all due respect, I'm not asking."

This got his attention quickly. He stopped looking at the papers on his desk and glared up at her, his eyes dark and menacing through the pipe smoke. He looked hard at the badge and then chuckled.

"Why'd they send a woman?"

She knew he was simply trying to get under her skin. So she let the comment slide right off of her back rather than exchanging verbal blows with him.

"You can just be cooperative," she said, "and this won't take much time at all. But if you'd rather a man come to question you, I can see to it. Only then, a lot more attention is going to be drawn to the situation and—"

"And what situation is that, exactly?" Albrecht asked. He placed both hands on his desk and leaned forward. Ava was certain he was going to spring to his feet at any moment and start shouting.

"I've been tasked with looking into the death of Alfred Perkins," she said. "And I've recently come into some information that links you to him." She waited for any sort of reaction from Albrecht, but there was none. "Did you know about his death?"

"Yes. I was told yesterday. Committed suicide or so it seems. Apparently, he jumped right off the top of the Chrysler Building."

"That's exactly right. And I learned today that you are one of the primary investors for the building. Is that correct?"

"It is," he said. "But if that's the only link you have, then you're wasting your time, little lady."

"Well, I do also happen to know that you were there, at the building, on the night of his death."

Albrecht did stand up this time. He stared her down, taking his pipe from his mouth and tossing it into an ashtray on his desk. "As were at least ten other people. Detective Gold, I suggest you get to your point quickly or I will indeed ask you to leave and I *will* make this as hard as possible on you. I have a very high-stress job and there are many people relying on me to ensure that they can keep their jobs. So please…get to the point."

Ava took the letter out of her pocket and slowly unfolded it. She turned it toward him so that the content was facing him. "Here's my point. Do you recall writing this letter, Mr. Albrecht?"

A flicker of worry passed across his stonelike face. "And how did you get that?"

"It was in Mr. Perkins's office. It was stashed away in a desk drawer, sort of hidden. Which makes me think he never worked with you on trying to get those investors pointed your way. Is that right?"

He shook his head, his eyes glued to the letter. "I won't discuss such matters without my lawyer present."

"Have it your way. But I have this letter, and it does plenty of talking without you there. I should also say that your refusal to answer my questions about your time at the Chrysler Building two nights ago is only going to make things look worse for y—"

Albrecht's right hand came up off of his desk, arcing through the air toward her face. She was so shocked by the action that the blow nearly landed. But Albrecht was not a fast man; apparently sitting at a desk all day did little for the physique.

Instead, Ava caught his arm, twisted it, and came around the side of the desk. She did it all in one fluid motion, and when she was standing by the side of the desk she wrenched his arm down. Albrecht cried out as she planted his hand on the desk. When he tried to pivot around her, she twisted again, applying pressure to his wrist and shoulder. He yelled out this time, in both frustration and pain.

"You release me right now!" he screamed. She was quite sure she sensed some embarrassment in his voice. After all, the woman they'd sent to talk to him was about an inch of pressure away from snapping his wrist or popping his shoulder out of socket.

"You ready to talk?" she asked.

"Go to hell."

In another quick motion, Ava stepped behind him and pulled his arm back. As Albrecht flailed around, she was able to also grab his other arm, pulling them both behind his back. He barely even had time to understand what was happening to him before she applied the handcuffs.

"You can contact that lawyer of yours from the precinct," she said.

"How *dare* you! You can't haul me out of here in handcuffs in front of the people I work with."

"Oh, we're well past that," Ava said. "That's something you should have thought of when you took a swing at a detective. A *female* detective at that."

She nudged him forward, toward the door, but he wouldn't move. "I'm not going anywhere," he argued.

"I can make this even more embarrassing for you."

"How can you even think about m—"

She drove an elbow into his lower back and when he hunched over, she caught him by his cuffed wrists and pulled up. When his back arched, she pushed forward and he went stumbling to the door. When he understood that he had no control at all in the situation, Albrecht stumbled on of his own accord.

He was quiet as she pushed him toward the elevators, even when they passed by his co-workers. She could feel the rage coming off of him, could feel the tightness in his muscles. And even before the elevator doors closed on them, she couldn't help but wonder how this little scene and arrest might affect her already shaky standing at her new precinct—and with her new partner.

CHAPTER TWELVE

When Ava hauled George Albrecht into the station half an hour later, she felt like there was a large, glaring spotlight on her. She'd not made it any more than ten feet inside the door before it seemed that every set of eyes were on her. And this time, because she was escorting a handcuffed man the stares lingered a bit longer than they had before. No one made much of an attempt to hide the fact that they were watching her or talking quietly about her behind their hands.

During her brief time to look the place over earlier in the day, she had a vague idea of where the interrogation rooms were located. She headed in that direction, noticing movement coming from where her desk was located. Out of the corner of her eye, she saw Pawlowski getting to her feet and starting to walk quickly in her direction. But at the last minute, Pawlowski seemed to think better of it. She simply stood there and stared, a confused and slightly frightened look on her face.

Even Albrecht seemed taken aback by the reaction of pretty much everyone in the station. He locked up for a moment, his knees going rigid. But Ava continued to push him along, not sure what she'd do if he decided to act on this moment of confusion and cause her to become physical in front of everyone.

Fortunately, that didn't happen. In fact, Albrecht even seemed to walk along a bit easier once she'd nudged him to get going again. She led him to the little hallway near the back of the room, not surprised to find the door to the first of three interrogation rooms opened up and vacant. She pushed him inside and closed the door behind them. A wave of relief washed over her when she could no longer feel everyone's eyes on her.

Albrecht grinned at her. "That wasn't the warmest of welcomes," he said. "It seems you have a knack for upsetting people, Detective Gold."

Ava had picked up a thing or two from listening to Clarence and having gotten these last few months of detective work under her belt. She had always been good at reading people, and though Albrecht seemed to be stubborn and difficult at his core, she thought she could probably figure out how to get him to cooperate as well. It would just take a bit of time. And based on the stares and murmurs she'd received upon coming through the door with Albrecht, she wasn't sure how much time she'd have.

"This can all be cleared up quickly," she said. "I only have a few basic questions for you. Questions I could have asked in your office if you hadn't tried to hit me."

"I want my lawyer present before I speak with you."

She eyed him, recalling how he'd seemed very worried about being carted out in front of his co-workers. Sure, that scene would start a little brush fire of rumors, but she wondered if she could lead him to believe it could all be salvaged—the situation, his reputation…everything.

"Sure thing," she said. "I can have someone arrange that for you. Or you could work with me for about five minutes and try to clear this all up. No lawyers means no unnecessary length to all of this. It can be written off as an unfortunate incident instead of a prolonged arrest situation where you were handcuffed and felt that you were in such danger that your lawyer needed to be present."

Albrecht said nothing, but his eyes wandered a bit as he considered it. Ava decided to keep pressing, trying to work her way through his worries and stubborn attitude.

"All I need to know is what you did on the night you were there to get the tour. I need to know that and what sort of interactions you had with Alfred Perkins in the days leading up to his death. The letter…it sounds pretty damning, and if you drag this out, it's going to look *very* bad for you."

"Don't you dare threaten me," Albrecht said. "With the hell I've been through these past few weeks, do you really think some misguided threats by a dizzy dame detective are going to make me sweat?"

"If you have nothing to hide, you have no reason to *not* answer my questions."

"Are you serious? You came into my office and essentially told me that I'm a suspect in a man's death."

"You're correct. That's my job. I found some clues, including the letter, that led me to think you might have something to do with it. Or, at the very least, have some information that could help me get to the bottom of—"

He was interrupted by the door opening behind her. When she turned to see who would possibly find it fitting to interrupt her, she saw

Captain Miller there. He sized up the room, his eyes going wide and alarmed when they fell on George Albrecht. He looked away from Albrecht at once, his gaze instantly boring into Ava.

There were perhaps three awkward seconds of silence before Miller was able to find his voice. "Detective Gold, I need to have a word with you, please."

She thought of arguing her case, of explaining why she had Albrecht here. But the last thing she needed was added friction her first day under Miller's eye—no matter how in the right she felt herself to be.

Without saying a word, she stepped outside of the interrogation room and into the hall. As Miller joined her, Ava watched as another officer quickly moved to take her place. It was a middle-aged man that looked very nervous and in a hurry. Ava assumed this man was being sent in as a form of damage control. And if that were the case, she also expected that she was going to be lectured and corrected by Miller.

He said nothing as he started walking down the hall, in the direction of his office. Ava followed behind him, once again feeling the eyes of the precinct on her. She noted that Miller was doing a decent job of making it appear that he was not upset but she could sense it coming off of him. This was especially true when he held his office door open for her and she passed by him to step inside. He closed the door behind them, sat down behind his desk, and wasted no time.

"Detective Gold, do you have any idea who that man is?"

"The one I brought in for questioning?"

"Yes."

"George Albrecht. He's an investor with Fulton and Donner Enterprises. He's also one of the primary heads of the investment projects that are helping to finance the construction of the Chrysler Building."

"It's nice that you know who he is, but it makes *absolutely* no sense that you would have him here, handcuffed in an interrogation room."

"He took a swing at me and refused to answer questions pertaining to a potential murder investigation," Ava said.

This clearly shocked him, and Miller spent several more minutes trying to find the right words to use next. "Why did he take a swing at you?"

"I don't know. If I had to guess, it's because a female was daring to ask him questions."

"Wait...back up, though. Why were you even trying to ask him questions?"

Once again, Ava showed the letter she'd found in Perkins's office. Miller read over it and then set it down on his desk. He rubbed at his chin in a thoughtful sort of gesture and then shook his head.

Before he could say anything, Ava pressed on. "There was also a bit of evidence at the scene of the so-called suicide of Alfred Perkins. A series of prints in the dust and debris that even the foreman said was very likely not that of a construction worker. And there's also the added fact that Albrecht himself has admitted to being at the Chrysler Building on the night of Perkins's death."

"All of that may be true," Miller said. "But it's a very flimsy trail at best. Not only that, but George Albrecht isn't just any old Joe off the street. Not only is he exceptionally wealthy, but he also happens to be friends with Walter Chrysler."

"So because of his friends and influence, he's made exempt from any criminal investigations, including murder?"

"Not all of them...but certainly ones where all signs clearly to point to a death being a suicide." He sighed and then looked her in the eyes. She was relieved to see what she thought was something like understanding He knew she was only doing her job, but she had not let power and influence blind her. To her, a man with wealth and power held no additional privileges than anyone else. "Has he asked for his lawyer?" Miller asked.

"Yes."

"And have any of these clues or links you've found concretely and without a doubt link him to Perkins's death?"

It was a good question—and one laced with many traps if she didn't answer it succinctly. "No, sir. They all seem to point to his involvement, but nothing nails him to the death without fail."

"Then I want you to walk back in there in about five minutes and let him go."

"But, sir, you can't let—"

"Officer Burke is currently making sure he won't press charges. After that, you *will* apologize to him and then release him."

Disappointment welled up inside of her and she had to bite back several arguments. At the base of it all, though, she knew why Miller was going this route. She didn't agree with it at all, but she did understand it. She also knew that this situation would be no different back at her old precinct. Minard would have reacted the same way. And as for Frank…well, Frank would have probably stopped her from bringing Albrecht in at all. Or, rather, he would have tried as hard as he could have.

"Look, Detective Gold, I knew this was a risk we'd take having you here. Captain Minard had expressed some concerns that you sometimes rub people the wrong way…sort of roll right over people if you feel strongly about something. And while you've not rolled over anyone in this situation—not exactly—you do need to keep behind a certain line when it comes to men like George Albrecht."

"Is that a line that says wealthy men are above the law?" Ava asked.

"As a detective in New York City, you know that's not the case," Miller said. "But you also know that it's a fine line."

She nodded firmly, not trusting herself to say anything else. But as she picked the letter back up from Miller's desk, she couldn't help but sneak in one last comment. She held the letter up with one hand and tapped at it with the other.

"Fine," she said. "But I want you to remember this letter. I want you to remember that I tried actually digging deeper into a case when everyone else was willing to look away and rule it a suicide."

She crammed the letter back into her pocket and left his office. This time, it seemed that hardly anyone was watching her. She couldn't help but wonder if everyone was doing their best *not* to look now that Miller had gotten directly involved. Whatever the case, she marched back to the interrogation room. The door opened and Officer Burke stepped out moments before Ava approached. He said nothing to her, just gave a sympathetic little nod, and hurried off on his way.

Ava waited by the door. She wondered what Frank would tell her in a moment like this. As she reached for the doorknob, she found herself missing him terribly. She felt it like a quick stab to the heart and then it was gone—only to be replaced by the embarrassment and anger she felt as she stepped into the interrogation room to let George Albrecht go.

CHAPTER THIRTEEN

The release of George Albrecht went much smoother than Ava expected. Not another cross word was spoken by the man during the entire process. It went so easily that as she watched him walk through the front doors, Ava couldn't help but wonder how this entire ordeal might come back to bite her.

When she was back at her desk, she was once again aware of the other officers looking at her. She was sure there would be plenty of gossip and shared laughs at her expense when everyone's shift was over. Wondering when that might be, Ava checked her watch and was shocked to see that, somehow, it was only 2:50 in the afternoon.

Being that the Alfred Perkins case was the only thing she had to occupy her time, Ava found herself unsure of where to go next, of what steps to take. She supposed she could continue to go down the list of names on Perkins's client list, but that seemed potentially like a bad idea given what had just happened with Albrecht. So, with no other avenue to pursue, Ava decided to check in on the status of that photograph request for the suspicious prints atop the Chrysler Building. Though even as she got up to hunt down some information, she doubted the request would go anywhere. It was becoming quite clear that this case was going to be ruled a suicide. It was confusing because she didn't see why she'd been moved out here to get stuck in a case that already had a predetermined outcome. Was she being punished in some way? Had Chief Freemantle and Captain Minard really sent her out here as punishment, only disguising it as a reward and opportunity? Had they had their fill of the city's most infamous woman detective, as well as the blooming relationship she was striking up with Frank Wimbly?

Also, she had no idea who to even ask for an update on the photo request. That meant she'd have to track down Pawlowski—and based on her reaction to Ava bringing in Albrecht, she doubted her new partner would even want to speak with her.

She searched the building over and found her pretty quickly. She could hear Pawlowski's stern but soft voice coming from inside the break room. It was accompanied by low, almost whispered male voices. One of them was chuckling in a way Ava thought sounded a little devious.

She stepped into the break room hesitantly. She figured if there was already a bit of quiet revelry taking place, her little mix-up with Albrecht was likely the reason. When she stepped in, she noticed that there were three male officers, two of whom were standing very close to Pawlowksi.

At first, Ava thought the group was huddled together laughing and gossiping about what had happened with Albrecht. Maybe the jokes had already started, and her new partner was leading the charge. But then Ava noticed the hardened look on Pawlowski's face and understood what was happening. Pawlowski's face had gone a shade of red in the cheeks and her eyes were like little flecks of stone.

And then Ava saw one of the men reach out to slap Pawlowski on the rear end. To her credit, Pawlowski tried to dodge it while reaching out to punch the man in the arm. All this did was give one of the others an opening to playfully slap her on the other side of her rear.

"I said let me out of here," Pawlowski said through gritted teeth. "Just…*move.*"

"We will," the man that seemed to be the ringleader of the group said. "I just need a little kiss. Or you show us some skin. Just a peek."

There was quiet laughter at this, during which one of the men happened to look over to the door, probably to make sure no one was seeing their vile little display. He looked alarmed at first but then smiled when he realized it was Ava, nudging the man next to him.

"Look at this," he said. "It's double the fun."

Pawlowski also looked over and the red in her face brightened with embarrassment and shame.

"You three have a very strange definition of fun," Ava said, finally stepping completely into the room. She could have turned and walked away, but she figured she was now a part of this because she'd witnessed it. And she'd been where Pawlowski was…she'd been there before and knew what it felt like. And she'd be damned if she would stand silently by.

"No, we know what fun is for sure," the leader said, taking a step toward her. "You give me a few minutes alone in a dark room with you, and I'll show you."

"Alone with you?" Ava said. "Yeah, it would *have* to be a dark room."

"Sam," one of the other said in a joking tone from behind him. "Don't you know? That's Ava Gold."

"I know who it is. But she's not anything special. Just another dame, trying to be something she's not in a world where she doesn't belong."

"What world is that?" Ava asked. "A man's world? A world where it takes three men to corner one woman in a break room just to cop a feel?"

The leader—Sam, apparently—smiled. "You know…I don't know how they handled broads down at your old precinct, but here, they're nothing but maids. Pretty little things to look at and send off on errands. So…let me be the first to welcome you to—"

He reached out to place a hand on her hip as he spoke. When he did, Ava grabbed his arm, pulled him forward, and pushed him hard. At the same time, she extended her foot out, tripping him. The result was Sam sprawling forward and hitting the ground. When he hit, he hit *hard.* She could hear the breath go rushing out of him.

She quickly wheeled around, sure that at least one of the other men would come to their friend's recue, posturing and trying to look strong, but both of them were frozen in place. One of them looked like he wanted to laugh at the situation but thought better of it. Feeling certain that neither of them were going to cause a problem, she turned back to Sam.

She turned just in time. He was on his feet and storming toward her. She wasn't sure if he'd be so brazen to actually try attacking her, but she wasn't about to take any chances. She assumed a defensive position, ready for anything. Sam apparently saw this as an invitation because he did indeed come for her. He extended his hand back, bringing a hard slap around. Ava ducked it easily, grabbing his arm in the process and swinging him hard to the left. He stumbled, collided with a chair behind the small table in the center of the room, and went to the floor once again.

"God, Sam," one of the other men said. "Stay down. Don't keep embarrassing yourself."

Ava wasn't so sure Sam would heed the advice, and she also knew that she was already flirting with disaster by her first two defenses. Taking the smarter, high road, she left the break room. She looked behind her quickly, making sure Pawlowski was taking advantage of the situation and also making an escape.

Ava supposed it would be smart to get moving. Staying in the building would only provoke Sam and the last thing she needed was a loud confrontation in front of everyone. Even though she felt she was in the right, she was not only a woman but a new face in the precinct. So she knew how that would go—and it would not be in her favor. She went to the front doors and headed out onto the street, having no real idea what her next step should be.

Before she made it all the way down the stairs and could sort out her thoughts, she heard her name called out from behind her. It was a woman's voice, and she sounded angry.

"Gold!" Pawlowski said. "Wait just a minute!"

Ava turned to see Pawlowski coming down the stairs. She looked not only angry, but maybe a bit embarrassed as well.

"What is it?" Ava asked.

"What the hell was that?"

Ava was shocked at first but quickly came to understand the situation. By essentially rescuing Pawlowski from the three men, she'd embarrassed her. Now she'd seem like the weaker of the two and no one would take her seriously. Everyone would see her as the poor little lady officer that needed another woman to swoop in and save her.

"I overreacted," Ava said, feeling silly for needing to apologize for standing up for another woman. "I can't stand to see men think they can just rule over women like that. And you looked uncomfortable and overwhelmed, so I—"

Pawlowski got right up in Ava's face, so close that their noses were nearly touching. "I don't need you to fight my battles for me."

Triggered by Pawlowski getting in her face, Ava was unable to keep control of her temper or her tongue. "Really? Because it seemed like those three were a little much for you. Or do you enjoy being groped like that?"

She could see the hurt and anger flashing in Pawlowski's eyes. She was also aware that if they stood there much longer, they were certainly going to attract unwanted attention.

"I didn't want you here," Pawlowski said. "But I tried to stay quiet and be the good little obedient woman. Seen and not heard, you know."

"And you're fine with that? Being only something to look at and not respected?"

"Of course I'm not," Pawlowski said, raising her voice. "You just…mind your own business while you're here, Gold. We're partners for now and I have to live with that, but you're not my protector."

And before Ava could respond to this in any way, Pawlowski turned and started back up the stairs. Ava watched her go, unable to *not* feel a little sympathetic. Maybe she *had* overstepped. After all, she knew what it was like to be the only woman in a precinct. She knew the obstacles and hardships Pawlowski faced every day. And yes, sometimes having someone save you from it was a burden more than a blessing.

Ava looked at the front door, and then to her watch. Her shift would be over in about forty-five minutes. She figured she could go back inside and debrief with Miller. Or she could head back out on the streets and try to scratch up more information on Perkins and his business with people associated with the Chrysler Building. Then again, with the way things had gone with Albrecht, she was a little hesitant to revisit it all in that moment.

"To hell with it," she muttered.

She turned away from the doors and started walking to the right. At first, her thoughts were indeed on Perkins and where else she may be able to look in order to get more details on what had truly happened to him. But within just a few steps, her thoughts went elsewhere Perhaps it was because of the stress and drama of the past ten minutes or so, or just because of the sudden change to her routine that she hadn't quite processed.

Whatever the reason, she started looking for a cab. And as she kept her eyes on the streets, she reached into the pocket of her jacket. There, she found the familiar shape she'd been carrying around since yesterday, thumbing the edges and wondering where it might lead her.

She was about to find out. She felt the matchbook in her hand, the words The Ash Lodge written on the front. But before she hunted down that particular location, there was another stop she needed to make first.

CHAPTER FOURTEEN

While she knew dishonesty was definitely not the best way to make an impression at a new precinct, Ava was fully prepared to tell Miller that the last half an hour or so of her shift had been spent looking for leads in the Perkins case. She felt confident there was no way he'd be able to find out what she'd really been up to—which was looking into what she felt might be the final pieces of her husband's stagnant murder case.

The cab dropped her off in front of the abandoned building where she'd found Jim Spurlock the day before. She was still unnerved by just how close she'd come to nabbing the bastard. That feeling of anxiousness and anger started to sizzle in her heart as she walked around to the back of the building. She doubted anyone would be there today after she'd busted in the day before. She was fine with that; she'd left the place so quickly yesterday that she hadn't had time to properly look around. She'd grabbed the matchbook on something of a whim and now wondered if there would be other clues that had been left behind.

When she entered through the back door, she was surprised to find that someone had been back. The place had been cleaned up, the scattered cards and poker chips collected from the floor. There was no sign that this little dusty back room had recently been used as a makeshift gambling parlor, and definitely no sign that she'd been here in a physical altercation that had nearly ended with the capture of Spurlock.

The fact that *someone* had been here in the last twenty-four hours or so put Ava on high alert. She glanced around the room, noting that there were several places someone could have hidden if they'd heard her coming: behind an old counter along the back wall, in a small closet-like room directly in front of her, or down the short hallway to her right that led to the central part of the building. Still, the place was so immaculately cleaned that she wondered if someone had swooped in, took all of their stuff, and relocated. She didn't think Spurlock was tied up with the mob but she also didn't think it was outside the realm of possibility that he was behind some sort of illegal, movable gambling organization.

She walked to the center of the empty room, still able to smell the lingering scent of smoke and sweat from the night before. She couldn't help but wonder how long Spurlock had used this place as a makeshift hub of operations. Had it been long enough for him to have run here in hiding after killing Clarence and escaping the police? To think he'd potentially spoken of it here, in this room, made her feel sick to the stomach. Of course, it was all just speculation at this point and she saw no sense in working herself up over it.

As she started to consider looking the place over, wanting to check every nook and cranny this time, her hand slowly dipped down to the holstered sidearm at her hip—the .38 revolver she'd somehow managed to not use lethally in her line of work just yet, despite her often reckless behavior.

She started walking for the closet because it seemed like the most obvious spot to make a quick escape for anyone that had been alerted at the last moment, maybe by her footsteps approaching the back door. She walked to it and as she reached out for the knob, she heard motion behind her.

She wheeled around, hand nearly drawing her gun. But she froze at what she saw, her instincts kicking in.

There were two men standing in the hallway. They'd apparently been elsewhere in the building and had just happened to come into the back room. That, or they'd known she'd been there ever since she'd first stepped inside. Whatever the case may be, they both had guns and they both looked abundantly happy to see her. She was quite sure she remembered one from last night. He was a tall, skinny man with a well-trimmed beard. He wore a casual suit and currently had a .38 of his own aimed at her.

The other man sported a handgun she'd never seen before. It was sleek and somehow much deadlier than his partner's .38. He was wearing a plain white shirt and a pair of black pants.

"Detective Gold," the suited man said. "I don't know if you're very brave or just plain stupid."

"I was thinking the same thing about you."

In the silence that followed, she nearly pulled her gun. She decided not to, mainly because she figured if these men wanted her dead, they would have shot her already—probably even before she'd turned around to face them. But if she *did* draw and they got antsy, there was a very good chance at least one of them would open fire.

Ignoring Ava's jab, the suited man sneered at her and asked, "Why are you here, Detective Gold?"

"Looking the place over."

"Why, exactly?"

Rather than answer, Ava tried another avenue. Even though she was outnumbered and had not been able to arm herself before coming under gunpoint, she had to somehow assert herself. "You geniuses understand that you're aiming guns at a member of the NYPD, right?"

"If you think we care, you're dumber that I thought. Now, come along like a nice little broad, and we'll be done with this soon enough."

Both men had taken a few steps forward, not fully out of the hallway. There were perhaps fifteen or twenty feet between Ava and the two goons. And as they took yet another step forward, that distance continued to shrink.

"Come along where?"

This time, it was the scrawnier one that answered. "We know you're trying to get your hands on Mr. Spurlock. So we're just going to take you to him. I think he might even be happy to see you."

"Maybe you just tell me where he is," Ava said. "I'll go see him myself. I don't need escorts."

"Let's just go ahead and put a stop to this right now," the suited man said. "Put it like this: you're either going to come with us right now, or you're not leaving this building." With a devious smile, he added: "It's not like we've never killed a copper before."

Ava did her best to size up her options. There weren't many—in fact, there were pretty much *zero* favorable ways out of this. So she was going to have to play it by ear…maybe let them feel as if they were in control (because really, that was the case here) and hope an opportunity presented itself.

She nodded and slowly moved her hand away from her holster. "Okay. Fine. But where are we headed?"

"Wouldn't you like to know?" the scrawny one said.

"You'll see soon enough," the suited man said. "And man, oh man, will Mr. Spurlock be happy. He might even leave Ms. Zebra without question if he knows we have you."

The name was peculiar enough that Ava took note of it, figuring it could come in handy later on. *Ms. Zebra,* she thought, committing it to memory. *That's going to be easy enough to remember.*

"You came in the back door," the suited man said. "So let's head out that way. We've got a car in the back lot, and I want you to walk real slow to it. Open the door, get in the back. We'll be behind you the entire time. You try to run, I'll put bullets in your knees. You try to draw that gun of yours and try anything brave, you'll get the same. I'm not going to shoot you in your pretty head, though. No…Mr. Spurlock will want you alive. And I think as a reward, he'll let us have some time alone with you."

Both men snickered at this as the suited man pointed his gun briefly towards the door.

"Move your cute caboose," he said, still laughing.

With her hands still held out to the side, she did as she was asked. If they wanted her going across a parking lot to a car, that meant she had at least twenty or thirty seconds to figure a way out of this. If it was just one of them, she'd likely try pulling her gun as she got to the doorway that led outside. But with two guns on her, that was a fool's errand.

When she reached the door and passed through the doorway, the suited man went so far as to even nudge her in the lower back with the barrel of his gun. "See the car over there?" he said. "The Studebaker."

"Yeah."

"That's the one. Go."

The Studebaker was parked in the farthest corner of the lot, which seemed odd as there were only two other automobiles in the lot that contained roughly twenty spaces for other cars. She figured this was to keep the car as hidden as possible, not wanting it out in the open. She wondered if they were truly taken aback by her appearance yesterday and were now taking extra precautions whenever they went out. It made her wonder what Spurlock and his deviant little crew were really up to and what sort of crimes they were involved in. But the walk to the car also gave her time to reflect on how absolutely foolish she'd been to come out here. Has she truly expected to slip from the Perkins case back into the secret case she'd been looking into concerning her husband? And if she'd found something…then what?

It really had been irresponsible. No one knew where she was if something *did* happen to her. Not even Frank. The thought made her a bit more scared and profoundly sad.

As they neared the car, she thought she had an idea. It was risky, but it was truly the only one she had. She faked a small stumble, just to ensure the suited man was still directly behind her. When he once again nudged her with the gun—this time right between the shoulder blades—she got the confirmation she needed.

When they arrived the car, the suited man reached out and took her by the shoulder. "Hold it."

The second man hurried ahead of them and opened the door. This put something of a dent in Ava's already tenuous plan, but she had to do something. Once she got into the car, she had a feeling things would be a lot more difficult.

The suited man gave her a little shove once the door was open. "Get in."

She turned slightly to the side, as she would any other time she was about to get into a car. But, with the suited man's hand still on her shoulder, she made her attack. She knew it was risky and she was expecting a gunshot to sound out at any moment. But until it came, she knew she had to fight.

When she lifted her leg to get into the car, she instead sent the lifted leg out hard to the right. It slammed into the suited man's calf, causing him to stumble. The moment he was off balance, she grabbed him by the back of his head and pushed him forward as hard as she could. Her intent had been to have him strike the car door, but his resistance threw off her aim and made things much worse for him.

His face went slamming into the glass of the door. The glass shattered and the suited man screamed.

She had no time to see the results, though. The scrawny man was already dishing out a left-handed haymaker. As Ava's luck would have it, though, the screaming suited man was in his way. So not only was Ava able to sidestep the blow, but she also pivoted around both men to get a better defensive position. Just as the scrawny man's wildly off-target punch came to its end, Ava placed two rapid-fire right-handed jabs into his perfectly exposed left side.

As the man crumpled, Ava also kicked him hard in the right arm. He dropped his gun instantly which, as Ava thought about it, might mean nothing. The fact that he'd tried punching her rather than shooting her when he'd had the chance made her think that Spurlock had given them instructions to bring her in alive.

To make sure she would have ample time to get away, Ava delivered one last blow—a punch that took the scrawny man directly in the side of the head. He hit the pavement hard but it was the screams of the suited man that really brought the moment home. Ava finally turned to him and grimaced as she started to run away. His face had gone through the glass, slicing open his forehead and placing a deep gouge in his cheek. She also saw a piece of glass the size of a coin sticking out of his face, just below his right eye.

Ava took off running. She knew she only needed to make it a block before she'd be able to camouflage herself in the flow of pedestrians and busy streets. And while she felt she'd dished out enough damage to make her escape, she also sense that the last two minutes may have drastically changed her life.

Once these men went back to Spurlock—who was now apparently actively on the lookout for her—there was no telling how hard they'd come after her.

CHAPTER FIFTEEN

It was 5:12 by the time Ava felt confident enough that she was out of any sort of realistic range of the two men she'd bested. She had a cab take her around the city for fifteen minutes, taking random lefts and rights until she finally asked the driver to take her to her apartment. But as she sat in the back of the cab, wired on adrenaline and the fear of what her actions may have just caused, Ava realized that there was no way she could take on the role of carefree mother for Jeffrey right now. She was too shaken, too off her game to be anything but a worried mess.

So at the very last moment, she leaned forward and gave the driver a different address—Frank's address.

When the cab dropped her off, she stood in front of the building for a moment. Before she even went inside, she thought about the last time she was here, knocking and not getting a response. She knew there was a very good chance she'd get more of the same this time around. It was barely after five, which meant he was probably still at work. She felt slightly conceited to think such a thing, but she imagined Frank would be burying himself with any work he could come by in order to keep his mind off of their workplace situation. He was clearly upset about the way things had worked out and she couldn't help but wonder if he viewed it as a hard strike against their relationship. In other words, speaking to her might be the very last thing he wanted right now.

But she was here now, so she figured she should at least try. She entered the building and, for the second time in less than twenty-four hours, climbed the stairs to Frank's apartment. As she came to the hallway and approached his door, the weight of just how badly she wanted him to be there settled in on her. Ever since they'd been given the news of their professional separation, she'd started to fear that he may just give up on the relationship. As she raised her hand to knock, she feared this even more; she feared that if he wasn't there again this time, it might very well be painting an accurate picture of what their relationship had become. Without a conversation, without argument, it could simply be over.

This was driven home when she knocked and there was no answer. She stood in front of the door, waiting, but somehow already knowing that he wasn't home. The night before, she'd felt the exact opposite. She'd had the sense that he had indeed been inside, but had chosen not to answer. She wasn't sure which feeling was worse, honestly. But God, she needed him to be there. The lingering nerves of having had a gun pointed at her less than an hour ago had her feeling out of sorts.

She knocked again, more out of obligation than hope. She stood there for two minutes, not sure where to go, what to do, how to react. Eventually, she slowly walked away, daring to hope that she might pass by him in the hallway or on the stairs as he came home from work. But she never spotted him. She toyed with the idea of heading down to the precinct and forcing him to speak with her but realized the sort of drama that would cause. There was no way anything productive would come out of that.

So in the end, she did what she'd intended to do from the start. She walked home. She rejected the idea of getting a cab, hoping the walk home would give her a chance to calm her nerves. It worked to some degree, though she couldn't help but wonder if Spurlock somehow knew where she lived. Or had there maybe been a third man back at his little abandoned building that had tracked her every move after she'd left?

These worries followed her home. And though they did diminish somewhat when she was in her apartment, wrapping Jeffrey in her arms as he started to tell her about his day, they were still there, echoing in the back of her mind. Conversation over dinner was brief and scattered. Her father did his best to ask about work without bringing up any indication of Frank, which was difficult when he'd become such a part of their afternoons. She supposed her father knew that there was *something* going on. He was a sharp man and had likely figured it out by now. She'd been reassigned yesterday and then Frank had not bothered to show up. That, plus her obviously frazzled mood, pretty much spelled it out for him.

After dinner, Jeffrey brought his deck of cards to the now-clean kitchen table. "Can we play some poker before bedtime?"

She smiled and tapped the kitchen table. "Shuffle and deal them out. You lose three times, and it's early bedtime for you. Is that too high-stakes for you?"

He shook his head eagerly as he slid the cards out of the pack and started to shuffle them. He did so slowly and with great care, still learning how to handle all of the cards. As usual, her father sat by Jeffrey, trying to coach him through certain moves and strategies. It was all just fun and entertaining enough to keep her mind off of Spurlock, Perkins, and even Pawlowski for a few minutes.

Jeffrey was able to survive through nine games before he lost three times (thanks to Roosevelt's assistance, of course) and was quite pleased with himself as Ava escorted him to bed. As they settled in and Ava lay down next to him, Ava realized just how tired she was. She supposed it might have a lot to do with the adrenaline that had rushed through her multiple times throughout the day: climbing up the Chrysler Building not once but *twice*, getting into a small physical confrontation at the new precinct, and then being held at gunpoint and taking down two of Spurlock's cronies. It was certainly a lot to endure in the course of a single day.

"Did you like your new workplace?" Jeffrey asked as he settled his head onto his pillow.

"Yeah, it was okay. It just takes a while to get used to a new place, you know?"

"Did you make any friends?"

She smiled at the naiveté of the comment and ran a hand through his hair. "Not yet, but we'll see."

"And you didn't get to see Mr. Frank today?"

"No. Not today."

She hugged him tight as the weariness overtook her. She sensed that she was about to fall asleep but was fine with it. Just a little nap. That would be fine. She'd drifted off from time to time right here in Jeffrey's bed several nights over the last few months—all of which had occurred after Clarence's murder.

She was faintly aware of the moment when Jeffrey fell asleep and then, just a short time later, allowed herself to doze off.

In the haze of her nap, she had a dream that had the strange, faint feel of a cloud. The images were there, the dreamlike narrative was there, but it was almost too detached for her sleeping mind to make sense of it.

In the dream, she was standing back at the top of the Chrysler Building. Only, when she looked across the exposed beams and to the open air beyond, it was not New York City that waited beneath her. Instead, there was a massive field of golden grass and weeds that stretched out as far as she could see. And standing directly on the edge of the floor, his back to her as he looked out at the breathtaking sight, was Frank.

"Pretty big out there, huh?" Frank asked.

"Frank…what are you doing?" Ava asked. "Step away from the edge. Turn around and talk to me. We'll…we'll be okay. Won't we?"

Slowly, Frank did step away from the edge. He turned around and looked at her and though it was indeed Frank's face, it bore the injuries she'd accidentally doled out to the suited man named Sam earlier in the day. Frank came walking forward, looking at her with a gashed forehead and cheek, a sliver of glass sticking out of his face just below his left eye.

"You really think so? I just…I don't know if—"

The floor shook, causing Frank to stumble back. Ava reached for him, but it was too late; he went falling over the side. The last thing Ava saw before gravity claimed him was his smile, as if he had wanted to fall the entire time.

Ava awoke with a start, her heart slamming in her chest. She momentarily clenched the mattress, her mind thinking she was still on top of the Chrysler Building for one terrifying moment. She looked beside her and saw Jeffrey, deeply asleep. She kissed him on the forehead and slowly got out of his bed. When she was out in the hallway, she checked her watch and saw that her nap had been a rather long one. It was 11:10 and she found that she was very much awake. After the fright the dream had given her, she didn't see herself going back to sleep anytime soon.

She did the only thing she *could* do, given the time and the increasingly tangled web she was creating for herself outside of her home. She went to her bedroom and lay down in the darkness. Staring up at the dark ceiling, she thought of all of the open threads of her life, of how quickly it had all changed, and how she might be able to tie it all up in a nice, neat bow.

She found no solutions, though. The best she could come up with was starting tomorrow with a mostly clean slate. And she thought everything needed to start by mending fences with Pawlowski—if her new partner would be willing to listen at all.

CHAPTER SIXTEEN

Ava arrived at the Seventeenth Precinct early the next morning, hoping to go over all of the files they had pertaining to Perkins one more time before having what promised to be a difficult conversation with Pawlowski. To her surprise, though, Pawlowski was already there. She was sitting at her desk, reading over a stack of papers. She glanced up at Ava for just a moment before turning her attention to the papers again.

"Good morning," Ava said as she sat down behind her desk.

"Same to you," Pawlowski said.

In the awkward silence that followed, Ava looked around the quiet precinct. She knew it wouldn't be this quiet for much longer. Within another half-hour or so, the officers that came in from the eight o'clock shift would fill it, moving around and going about their business and caseloads. Unable to stomach the quiet much longer, Ava tried her best to get the conversation started.

"Are you still mad at me?"

Pawlowski waited a moment, her eyes still on the stack of documents in front of her. After a while, she looked up and met Ava's gaze. "I am," Pawlowski said, "but not as mad as I was yesterday."

"That's a start."

"I guess I've just never been the sort to need someone to rescue me. I didn't ask for your help. I didn't cry out like a damsel in distress, but still…there you were. Looking back on it, I do appreciate the help. And it was *amazing* to see those busters get what was coming to them. Still, it was a little embarrassing." She shrugged and added: "You've been doing this long enough to know what I mean, right?"

"I know exactly what you mean. And I…I don't know. It just made me mad, and I reacted."

"You ever do anything like that at your old precinct?"

"A few times," Ava said with a slight smile. "Are we good here?"

Pawlowski considered it, still looking Ava over. Eventually, she nodded and said, "Yes. We're good. And with that…here's what I was able to pull from those other names on the client list we found in Perkins's office."

She slid the papers over to Ava in an almost disgusted way, as if she was very happy to get them off of her desk. Ava looked the papers over and found that there wasn't much there at all.

"I know," Pawlowski said. "There's not much there. They are all well-to-do businessmen and investors. I did also check their names against local obituaries and none of them have killed themselves."

"I wonder how we could find out if any of them are investing any money into the Chrysler Building."

"I doubt we can," Pawlowski said. "I checked on that request we put in for a photographer, and it's been denied. I know you don't want to hear it, Gold, but you're just about the only one that really thinks there might be foul play involved in this."

This didn't surprise her. In fact, she fully expected Miller to call them both into his office at some point during the day to tell them that he was killing the case and Alfred Perkins's death would officially be ruled a suicide.

"The letter to Perkins from Albrecht didn't seem at least a little strange to you?"

Pawlowski signed and gave Ava a *what-are-you-gonna-do* sort of look. "Yeah, it does raise the eyebrows, huh? But then again, you saw how Miller and the rest of the precinct reacted when you bought Albrecht in here, right? I'm telling you…unless you can find some sort of undeniable proof, this is going to be dead in the water really soon."

"How about you?" Ava asked. "Do you think it's still worth looking into?"

"I honestly don't know. I keep thinking about the prints we saw. Even the foreman thought they were odd. There's also the fact that Perkins really would have had no business in the building in the first place. There's a lot that doesn't add up for sure, but that's not going to be enough for Captain Miller to keep the case active."

"So how about we do everything we can before Miller kills it?" Ava said.

"I'm not sure what else there is to do."

Ave thought it over. She wasn't sure how revisiting the Chrysler Building would help, so that was out. She supposed going back to Perkins's office could be of some help, but digging through all of that paperwork was going to take a lot of time—and that was something they simply didn't have. It then occurred to her that they may already have a built-in shortcut for finding smaller bits of information.

"What about the wife?" she asked. "What about Stella Perkins?"

"She really wasn't too much help the first time, now was she?" Pawlowski said.

"But the last time we spoke to her, we didn't know about the connection to Albrecht. it might be worth asking her about some of his financial information…just to see if she knows any little details that might be worthwhile and hidden in all those binders of information in his office."

"That's a good point," Pawlowski said.

"And you know," Ava said. "If there *is* anything damning, wouldn't it almost make sense that he'd keep that information at home? If he's got financial ties to Albrecht that he didn't want people at his work finding out about, it would be foolish to keep it all at the office."

"Then why keep the letter there?" Pawlowski countered. "Sure, it was hidden and all, but still…"

It was a good point, and Ava had to admit that it didn't make much sense—unless he'd kept the letter close at hand in his work environment in the event he ever felt cornered or pinned in by Albrecht. If something like that ever happened, the letter was essentially proof that investors involved with the Chrysler Building were trying to snip investors from other sources.

The truth of the matter was that they just didn't have enough information to make any sort of informed theory. Hopefully, Stella Perkins would be able to help.

"Well, then, let's get going," Ava said. "Wouldn't it be very convenient if we just happened not to be here when and if Miller decided to kill the case?"

Pawlowski grinned, apparently enjoying Ava's slightly rebellious side. "Are you this devious back at your old precinct?" she asked, getting to her feet, and already heading for the doors.

"Every now and then," she said. And as she also got to her feet and started following behind Pawlowski to the doors, she couldn't help but think of Frank. He would have probably also been in agreement that sneaking out was the right move, and she wondered how he might handle this situation She missed his take on things, his rigid and by-the-book way of thinking. And as she and Pawlowski headed out to speak with Stella Perkins, she wondered what she might be missing in terms of this case without Frank by her side.

CHAPTER SEVENTEEN

Stella Perkins had seemed detached and almost bored the first time Ava and Pawlowski had visited, but Ava was pretty sure the grief of losing her husband had caught up with her since then. When Stella answered the door, she looked very tired. Her eyes were bloodshot, her hair was a mess, and she looked pale. At the same time, though, she looked almost pleased to see the two detectives at her doorstep.

"Agents…Gold and…I'm sorry, I don't remember your name, dear," Stella said, looking apologetically at Pawlowski.

"Pawlowski. It's okay. It's not really easy to remember. It's not like it rolls off the tongue or anything."

"Well, come in," Stella said. "Can I offer you come tea or something?"

"No, thank you," Ava said. "I do apologize for coming back by, but our hands are tied. Mrs. Perkins, may I speak bluntly?"

"Of course," she said. They'd all settled down around the long dining room table, Stella practically melting into her seat.

"Detective Pawlowski and I believe that we have found just enough speculative evidence to suggest that your husband did not kill himself But the simpler facts of the case all seem to point to that conclusion. Our concern is that if we can't come up with something undeniable, his death will officially be ruled a suicide and we'll be taken off the case."

"Yes…I feared as much. I'm happy to do anything I can to help."

"Well, we now have reason to believe that he was being contacted by some people that were working with investors for the construction of the Chrysler Building—that he was being asked to convince some of his company's investors to start pushing their money towards the construction and future investments in the property. So far, we have no evidence that Mr. Perkins was in fact doing this, but we know he was at least *asked.*"

"Does that surprise you?" Pawlowski asked.

"If you're asking me if he ever mentioned those connections, the answer is no," Stella said. "As I said before, Alfred never really talked to me about his work."

"Did he ever bring work home with him?" Ava asked.

"Yes, all of the time. I believe he often brought materials related to some of the bigger, more important clients."

"Does he have a room he used as an office?"

"Yes. Would you like to see it?"

"Yes, that could be a huge help," Ava said.

When Stella led them through the house, Ava once again noted how distraught the poor woman was. She moved like a phantom in her own home as she led them down a large hallway that ended at a closed door. When she reached out and opened it, Stella seemed to let out a sigh. Ava wondered if the door had been closed ever since her husband had died.

The door opened up onto a gorgeous yet simple office. A mahogany desk sat in the center of the room, and there were leatherbound books stacked on two small bookshelves behind it. The room smelled of old cigar smoke and a hint of leather. On the desk, two neat stacks of paper rested.

"If you're looking for financial information," Stella said, "you'll find it there, at the bottom of the second bookcase. I only know this because he had me fetch him notes and documents of all kinds."

"Would you allow us to look through them?" Pawlowski asked.

"Yes, anything you need. Help yourself."

Ava made her way over to the bookshelf Stella had mentioned and found a simple box tucked away alongside a few books as if it had been made to hide perfectly in that exact spot. She removed it and set it on Alfred Perkins's desk. Removing the lid, they found a few folders, the same size and style of the ones they'd seen at his office back at 40 Wall Street. They removed the folders, finding only four. Beneath them was a checkbook, which Stella found very interesting once they took it out.

"I've never seen that before," she said. "He'd had me go into this box a few times in the past, but there's never been a checkbook in there."

Stella then seemed to realize that staying in the office might not be the best idea in terms of trying to process everything or to stay out of the way of the detectives. She moved slowly back out into the hallway, looking like she was lost in her own home.

Pawlowski opened one of the folders. It had roughly thirty sheets of paper inside, all of which had numbers and dates typed on them. Ava opened the next folder and found more of the same.

"Any idea what we're looking at here?" Pawlowski asked.

"Not at all. But if the checkbook is in the same stashed-away box as these folders, they have to be related, right?"

"I'd say that's a safe bet."

Ava looked through the checkbook as Pawlowski continued looking through the financial records, both women trying to make sense of what they were seeing. Ava had always hated anything to do with numbers, so she found it frustrating. She did her best to switch her mentality, viewing the numbers as a puzzle to be solved rather than just a series of random numbers and figures.

She noticed right away that Perkins had done an exceptional job of keeping his records and finances straight. Everything in the checkbook's register was well-organized and recorded. And that's exactly what helped her to pinpoint the first oddity among it all. She double-checked the numbers to make sure she was correct before sharing it with Pawlowski.

"Here's something odd," Ava said. "I've got four different transactions in the leger that aren't accounted for. The amounts are listed, but there's no designation." She pointed to the first of the four entries as she explained it. "He's sort of hiding transactions of money spent in other listed transactions. Right here, for example…when he subtracts this thirteen dollars for an exchange at the tailor's shop, there's an additional one hundred and fifty dollars missing in the checking account's total after he does the math. And then here's another example: the total in the account should be fourteen thousand and two dollars after this eight-hundred-dollar real estate payment, but instead, it's a little under thirteen thousand nine hundred. He's buried some other expense in that listing…unless he's just *really* bad at math."

"Based on all of these figures I'm seeing, I don't think that's the case," Pawlowski said.

Stella's voice spoke up quietly from behind them. "No…Alfred was very good with numbers. He wouldn't make mistakes like those."

Ava turned to Stella and saw the confusion in her tired eyes. She hated to drag this out for the poor woman, but she felt that they were on the brink of a considerable discovery. "Mrs. Perkins, do you know where the primary checkbook is? The one he would use for home-and-family business?"

"He kept it in that box as well…though I had to move it yesterday to have my sister write a check to the funeral home. One moment…I'll get it."

As Stella made her way back through the house, Pawlowski spoke up. "Hold on…Gold? What was that first listing you pointed out? The one at the tailor? How much was missing?"

"One hundred and fifty."

"Is there a date?"

"The date he listed for the tailor was September third."

"Look at this," she said, slipping a sheet of paper from the second folder over towards her. "There's a listing right here of one hundred and fifty dollars, given a date of just a few months ago."

Ava still wasn't exactly sure what it might mean. But based on the scant information they had, it seemed that Perkins had been removing money from this checking account and keeping up with the money somewhere other than the check register.

"And look at this," Pawlowski said. She'd lowered her voice, likely so Stella wouldn't hear her.

But as she started to show Ava what she'd found, Stella came walking back into the office. Pawlowski went quiet and started focusing on the papers once again as Stella handed over a nicer, much larger checkbook.

"You're welcome to look it over," Stella said. "But I *would* like to know what you think you've found."

Ava wasn't sure if she wanted to share what she was suspecting because she didn't want to cause Stella any more pain; she certainly didn't want to provide her with a reason to think ill of her husband or to suspect him of any foul play.

"It's okay," Stella said. "I loved my husband and while he was a kind and loyal man, I have no illusions that he wasn't a little shady and shifty when it came to money. Let me remind you again…Alfred liked to go big on all things."

Pawlowski looked at Ava and shrugged. "Well," Pawlowski said, "this is only speculation right now, but I just discovered this." She showed both Ava and Stella the last item she'd found, the one she'd nearly mentioned before Stella had come into the room. "The listings on some of these pages seem to line up with totals taken out of the smaller checkbook that he didn't list in the register. More than that, though, there are a few instances in these papers where it appears he lists a few different accounts." She stopped and pointed to the series of numbers that could very well be bank accounts.

Absently, Stella opened the larger checkbook she'd just brought back into the room. She looked at the top of the first check in the book and pointed to the account number in the bottom left-hand corner. Ava was not at all surprised to see that it was different from the one Pawlowski had pointed out.

"What does it…?"

Apparently, Stella didn't see the point in finishing the question. Her face contorted a bit, and Ava was sure she was going to start crying rather soon. The widow shook her head and slowly backed away.

"Mrs. Perkins?"

She smiled faintly and made a shooing gesture. "Don't mind me," she said. "I'm just tired. And I don't have the strength to deal with something new right now. You ladies just…you do what you need to do."

"Will you be alright?" Pawlowski asked.

"Yes, I think I'll call my sister again…have her come sit with me. Thank you for all you're trying to do."

Ava and Pawlowski exchanged a tense look as Stella's footfalls disappeared down the hallway. They then looked back down to the two checkbooks and the listing of transactions that were apparently nowhere to be found in either book.

"This is a lot of paper to go through," Pawlowski pointed out.

"It is. And fortunately, we won't have to go through it all. Both checkbooks are from the same bank. The only difference is the account number."

"And there's no name on this second account."

"No worries there," Ava said, picking up the checkbooks and the folders. She placed them all back in the box and picked it up from the desk. "The bank can sort all of that out for us."

Pawlowski nodded enthusiastically as they started out of the room. Ava couldn't help but feel slightly encouraged, too. Shady financial deals in tandem with the note from Albrecht continued to paint a suspicious picture. And as they neared the sound of Stella Perkins weeping from her parlor, Ava felt that they owed it to this poor woman at the very least, to find out what truly happened to her husband.

<h1 style="text-align:center">CHAPTER EIGHTEEN</h1>

As Ava and Pawlowski entered the Second National Bank, another detail of the case occurred to Ava. It was quite obvious and in realizing it, she was ashamed for nearly missing it completely while they'd been back at the Perkins' residence. By Perkins listing each of his hidden transactions separately and then referencing another checking account, she assumed it meant that his hidden money wasn't being directed towards investment; from the way it looked, based on what they knew, it was being funneled into a secondary account. An account he'd been keeping up with in the secondary checkbook.

This did put a dent in the investment angle of the case, but Ava also knew it would be a mistake to rule anything out before speaking with the bank.

In her hurry to get to the counter and ask to speak with a manager, Ava nearly overlooked the quiet and morose atmosphere in the bank. It was a grand building, well-decorated, giving off the feeling of wealth and comfort. But at the same time, there was a pallor in the air that was unsettling. It was more like walking into a funeral parlor than a bank. Ava wondered if it was the same in all banks across the city as a result of the crash.

The detectives approached the first available teller, a woman that smiled widely but looked as if this might be the last place on the planet she wanted to be. "Can I help you ladies?"

"We'd like to speak with a manager, please."

The teller nodded politely, probably relieved that she could pass them on to someone else. "Give me just one moment, please." She stepped around the counter and marched out of the lobby, down a hall to their right. After disappearing into a door roughly halfway down the hall, she entered a room. Several seconds later, she came back out, that same smile on her face, and waved them on to follow her.

Ava and Pawlowski headed in that direction, passing by the teller as she headed back for the counter in the lobby. When they came to the door, they found it open and with a rotund, short man sitting at a large, cluttered desk. His office was decorated almost like a living room, comfortable and stylish. He beamed up at them, adjusting a pair of bifocals that sat slightly crooked on his nose. A small placard on the side of his desk read: **Donald Whetley.**

"Can I help you ladies?" he asked.

"I hope so," Ava said, slightly lifting the box she'd been carrying the entire time. As she sat it on the edge of Whetley's desk, Pawlowski took the opportunity to show her badge.

"I'm Officer Pawlowski, and this is Detective Gold," she said. "We're looking into a murder that we believe has been set up to look like a suicide. We believe we may have found enough evidence in the victim's financial records and work correspondence to further the case. But we need some help in terms of the financial records and checking accounts we've come across."

"Okay…" Whetley said, clearly confused and a bit alarmed. "What is the name of the deceased?"

"Alfred Perkins."

"Oh," he said, the name instantly registering with him. "Oh, my. I'm so sorry to hear this."

"Did you know him personally?" Ava asked.

"Not, not well. Just as a loyal client to the bank. And if you're here because you've been looking into his financial life, I assume you know he was relatively wealthy. So he was in and out of here quite a lot."

"Then it seems you would be in a good position to help us out," Ava said. As she started removing the papers and folders from the box, she did her best to catch him up, explaining what she and Pawlowski had found in Perkins's home office. When she was done, Whetley looked at the women with a perplexed expression.

"In other words," Pawlowski said, "we need to know where the hidden amounts are going. Based on what we see here in these folders, there's an entirely different account, but we don't know who owns it."

"I'm afraid that isn't information I can just hand out," Whetley said. "As I'm sure you can imagine, there was likely no name assigned to it for a reason. Perhaps it was for some personal matter that Mr. Perkins didn't want anyone to know about."

"Okay, then, how would the rightful owner of that account get money out if there's no name on it?" Ava asked.

"By providing the account number and proof of their identity."

Ava leaned forward sightly across the desk, and said: "You understand that we need to know this information so we can prove that a man—one of your clients as you pointed out, did not kill himself, right?"

Whetley looked shaken, probably because he'd never had a woman speak to him in such and angry and direct way. "Yes, yes…I understand that, but…it's our policy. I just can't…I…"

"Calm down there, Mr. Whetley," Pawlowski said. With a smile, she walked to the edge of the desk. When she approached Whetley, Ava nearly asked what she was up to but figured she'd let her new partner go with her gut. Ava took a single step back as she watched the peculiar scene unfold, though.

To Ava's shock, Pawlowski stood directly in front of Whetley. When she leaned closer, Ava was convinced that she was going to kiss him on the cheek. During the entire encounter, Whetley stood motionless, his face filled with confusion. But then, when Pawlowski whispered softly into his ear, that confusion turned to fear. His cheeks filled with red, which was odd because the rest of his face went pale.

Pawlowski only spoke for ten seconds or so. Ava could hear the whispering tone of her voice but couldn't make out any words. But when she finally pulled away, Whetley was clearly shaken. He habitually adjusted his bifocals and, though he couldn't look Ava in the eye, he also seemed afraid to look at Pawlowski.

When Pawlowski had stepped back, Whetley did his best to regain his composure. He smiled again, though it was not nearly as genuine as the one he'd offered when they'd first come into his office. "Yes, well," he said. "Let me go speak with one of our account specialists and see if I can get that information for you."

"Thank you," Pawlowski said brightly.

When Whetley was out of the room, Ava leaned in close to Pawlowski. "What the hell did you say to him?"

"I just let him know that his failure to help would lead to a few officers coming down and taking a look into the matter later on—that it could either be a lot of cops to make the bank look a little risky, or just us two sweet gals. I also said if he mentioned what I was whispering to him to you, I'd make sure he was personally investigated."

"That's a smart move. So…I suppose you're the villain and I'm the hero in this situation?"

"However you want to look at it."

The entire exchange seemed to shift their relationship in one pivotal moment. They were a very long distance away from being friends, sure, but there was trust and a sense of comradery between them now. It had been a joke, veiled as how they'd really felt at first…but communicating the joke itself had knocked down any remaining barriers. Even better, Ava thought, was that Pawlowski didn't feel the need to point it out or wax poetic about it. They accepted it for what it was with thin smiles and acknowledgment and nothing more.

They didn't have to wait long for Mr. Whetley to return. He came back less than two minutes later, shadowed by a man that looked a bit older. He was tall, dressed in a very nice, tailored suit, and looked just as nervous as Whetley. He had a single folder in his hand and when he set it on the desk in front of Ava and Pawlowski, he did a commendable job of not looking as nervous as he had upon entering the room.

"I'm so very sorry to hear that Mr. Perkins has passed," he said. "I believe these are the papers you'd be looking for in regards to his secondary personal account."

When Ava picked the folder up, the tall man stepped back as if he had no idea what to expect—either a polite thank you or a punch to the jaw. His puzzled expression made Ava think he might be expecting either one at any moment.

The folder consisted of just three sheets of paper. The first item of note in the top left corner was the account number—the very same one they'd found listed in Perkins's documents. Below that account number was a name: Kathleen Branson.

"Any idea who this is?" Ava asked pointing to the name.

"No," the tall man said. "All we know for sure is that it was an account set up for her."

Ava studied the numbers and listings in the documents. Within a few seconds, she recognized several listings from Perkins's records. And it quickly became clear where the missing funds from Alfred Perkin's records had been going. That money had been funneled into Kathleen Branson's account.

Ava quickly flipped through the pages to see if she could determine just how much money had been given to Branson. Near the bottom of the page, though, something changed. Rather than a series of funds put into the account, she saw quite a lot taken out. In fact, at the very bottom, the account's total was $0.05. This was a drastic difference from the highest amount in the records, which was at the top of the same page and listed as $16,300.

The date of the last listed withdrawal or expenditure was just six days ago.

"So this account is completely wiped out?" Pawlowski asked.

"Yes, it seems that way," Whetley said.

"Do you have an address for her?"

"I believe so," the tall man said. As he thumbed through the pages and scanned them, he seemed calm, perhaps relaxing in the presence of order and numbers. "Here," he said, "is the address of Mr. Perkins. I am assuming this secondary address would be for Ms. Kathleen Branson."

Ava studied it to commit it to memory. Meanwhile, Pawlowski simply grabbed a piece of paper from Whetley's desk, as well as an elegant pen, and scribbled it down.

"Thanks for your help, gentlemen," she said. She returned the pen to the desk and gave Whetley a particularly stern gaze. "Detective Gold, I think we should leave these men to their work, what do you say?"

Without waiting for an answer, Pawlowski headed out of the office, stuffing the paper with the address into her pocket. Ava managed to keep stride with her as they walked back through the lobby and the front counters.

"That was well-played," Ava said. "Maybe a bit mean and pushy, but well-played."

"You've got to be like a hurricane sometimes," Pawlowski said. "Let them feel the strong winds for a while, then hit them and get out before they have time to survey the damage."

Ava couldn't help but smile at the analogy as they made their way back out onto the streets. The morning traffic was lighter on both the streets and the sidewalks as it thinned out while people began to arrive at work. And with another lead stuffed into Pawlowski's pocket, Ava dared to hope the morning might finally bring them some luck.

CHAPTER NINETEEN

The address given for Kathleen Branson led them to a very nice apartment building in Eastern Manhattan. There was even a doorman out front, nodding politely to Ava and Pawlowski as they made their way inside. The apartment lobby had the build and design of a refined office building, though it was small and compact—perhaps, Ava thought, to give its residents the feeling of not only safety, but exclusivity.

According to the bank records, Ms. Branson lived in Apartment 2B. Ava and Pawlowski took the stairs, and though it was only one single flight, Ava couldn't help but wonder if she'd be resenting even the slightest flight of stairs for a good while thanks to her trips to the Chrysler Building.

Pawlowski knocked on the door and they waited in silence. The entire building, not just the apartment beyond Branson's door, was relatively quiet, making it easy to acknowledge that there were no footsteps or other movements. Pawlowski knocked again, though Ava was pretty sure her partner had come to the same conclusion: Kathleen Branson was not home.

"What do you think?" Pawlowski asked. "I was the hurricane back at the bank. I think it's your turn." She gestured toward the door as she spoke.

"You mean just force our way in?"

Pawlowski shrugged. "I think there's enough viable reason for it."

Ava considered this for a moment and came to the same conclusion. What they knew for certain is that Alfred Perkins had been secretly making deposits into a secondary (or maybe even lower than that) account for a woman named Kathleen Branson. The final withdrawal, which had emptied the account, had come just a few days prior to Perkins's death. And while they knew nothing about Branson, it was fairly easy to paint a picture of a likely scenario.

If Branson was an acquaintance of Perkins's that no one knew about and Perkins had been giving her money on the sly, it was safe to assume she was some sort of mistress. And if the stock market crash had affected Perkins's ability to continue funneling her money, another safe assumption was that it had probably made her angry. A woman with expensive tastes that had been relentlessly pampered was not going to take such a quick and drastic change very well.

But mad enough to murder? Ava wondered. She supposed there was only one way to find out.

"You know how to pick a lock?" Ava asked.

"No. You?"

Pawlowski shook her head. Simply because she felt it was the most sensible thing to do, Ava reached out and grabbed the handle. She turned it, fully expecting it to be locked. So when it turned over easily in her hand, she was surprised. She hesitated for a moment before turning the knob the rest of the way. The door opened easily.

"Lucky for us, huh?" Pawlowski said.

"Maybe." Ava wasn't so sure. The fact that the door was unlocked actually made her a little uneasy. Still, she stepped inside with her hand hovering near her sidearm. Pawlowski came in behind her, clearly not as troubled.

The door opened up on a simple and quaint living area. A couch sat against the far wall, an ornate rug on the floor. Other than a small end table by the couch, adorned with two books, there wasn't much else to see. They stepped into the kitchen and found it just as sparse; a small table with two chairs and a simple icebox were pushed against the left wall, allowing easy passage into a hallway that led to a bathroom and an elegant bedroom.

In the bedroom, the bed was made and a small bureau sitting on the opposite wall was bare. As Ava stepped into the bedroom, processing the rest of the place, she started to realize that it had a very undisturbed feel. She walked over to the bureau and studied it closely. On the surface along the top, there were the faintest trace amounts of white powder, the sort women often use on their face. She then checked the three drawers within the bureau and found them all empty. Still, one of them offered the ghostlike scent of old perfume. Someone had been living here, sure enough, but Ava had the hunch that they hadn't been here for a while.

"Sort of spooky," Pawlowski said.

"Yeah, a bit," Ava agreed. "The empty drawers and lack of—"

A third voice interrupted her. It came from the front of the apartment, by the front door. "Hello?" an older man's voice said. "Who's in there?"

Ava gave Pawlowski a *stay here* gesture as she made her way back into the hall. Before the living room or the speaker came into view, she announced herself. "I'm Detective Ava Gold, with the New York Police Department. Who are you?"

There was a moment of silence before she got an answer. By then, though, she'd entered into the kitchen and could see the man as he answered. Ava guessed him to be in his late fifties. He was dressed in basic work clothes—a white shirt and a pair of well-worn pants. There was a bit of grime on his right forearms and a sheen of sweat on his brow.

"I'm Andrew Craft," he answered. "I own the building and take care of maintenance." He frowned and showed off the grime and dirt on his forearm. "As you can see. My doorman downstairs told me he let you two in and then I came up and saw this door open. Is there something I can do to help you?"

"We're looking for a woman named Kathleen Branson," Ava said. "We were given this address for her last known."

"Well, unless a miracle has occurred in the past two days or so, I imagine this *would* be her last known address."

"What do you mean?" Ava asked Behind her, Pawlowski stepped into view. After a quick introduction, Craft went on.

"She lived here for about a year. Maybe a little less, I'm not quite sure. Always paid her rent on time, always quiet and respectful. But two days ago, I had to kick her out. She was two months behind on her rent and refused to pay. She kept making excuses. But as you know, times are hard right now and I can't waste an apartment on someone that isn't going to pay. So I had to evict her."

"Did she pay you herself, in person?" Ava asked.

"A few times. Usually it came to my own apartment, in an envelope. Always on time, until a few months ago. I figured she was falling on hard times just like everyone else and I hated to kick her out, but..." He shrugged, and Ava could sense some sincere guilt in the gesture.

"Mr. Craft, the door was unlocked when we arrived. Were you aware of this?"

"Yes, I was aware. I left it unlocked for the locksmith that's due to show up this afternoon. Once he changes the locks and I strip her bed and give the floors a good scrubbing, the apartment will be ready for someone else."

"Any chance you know where she was going when she left here?"

Craft shook his head, frowning. "Sorry, but no."

"Did she have anyone helping move things out?" Pawlowski asked.

"Not that I'm aware of. She did it on her own, a little at a time. I even volunteered to give her a hand, but she refused it. She was angry at me, I suppose. She'd seemed angry for a while, really. She kept complaining about how she'd have to live on the streets with all the riff raff and how she'd have to sell all of her belongings." He chuckled and said, "The last time I actually spoke to her, she was near tears because she said she'd pawned a pair of diamond earrings that were very special to her just to be able to pay that last month's rent. You know…before the bottom fell out on us all."

"Do you know of any family members or friends she maybe had over on occasion?" Ava asked.

"Sorry, no. She was somewhat private, I suppose. I only spoke to her when I happened to cross paths with her in the building. On those occasions, she was more than happy to talk but that was the extent of my relationship with her."

"I   see.   Well,   thank   you   all   the   same." "Sure." Craft paused, considering something, and then asked: "Say, is she in some kind of trouble I should know about?"

"No, sir," Ava said, though she honestly wasn't so sure herself. "We're just hoping she can answer some questions regarding a case we're working on."

"Oh. Sorry I wasn't any more help."

Ava took one last look around the apartment, making sure they'd missed nothing. But based on what Craft had told them, Branson had likely moved out anything that would have been of any interest.

Slightly defeated, Ava and Pawlowski left the apartment and headed back out onto the street. They stood in front of the building for a moment, both processing everything they'd just learned.

"I assume you noticed that Branson's eviction lines up with the same day of Perkins's death, right?" Pawlowski asked.

"I did. And I also can't help but wonder if the money he'd been putting in that account stopped as a result of the market conditions. If I recall, the last deposit was from about a month ago. They seemed to have stopped after that."

"You think she got hot-headed about not getting that stream of cash and murdered him? Pawlowski asked.

"I know it seems a bit much, but it's worth considering. The main question goes back to the way he was killed. Why would she get him to go to the Chrysler Building?"

"Yeah, and then all the way up to the top."

"We need to find this woman and talk to her," Ava said.

"All we have is a name and a shady connection to a dead man," Pawlowski pointed out. "Finding a dame like that in this city is going to be impossible."

"Maybe not," she said. "Mr. Craft mentioned that she had pawned off diamond earrings recently."

"Yeah?"

"So we go to every pawn shop we can find. I think we can probably eliminate the smaller, grimier ones right away. If Kathleen Branson was used to the finer things and being pampered with money, I doubt she'd stick her head in places like those."

"I think you're on to something there, Gold. How well do you know the pawn shops around here? Even by eliminating the crummy ones, there's going to be a few to check into."

"Well, I'd say we can split up, but that could end up wasting time with us trying to meet back up."

"The we'll just have to move quick," Pawlowski said. "I imagine Captain Miller has started looking out to the desks for us by now."

Ava didn't like the thought, so she started moving right away. She'd passed several pawn shops in the last few days but couldn't for the life of her remember their names or where they were. They had no choice but to walk the streets, looking for pawn brokers and hoping they could slip into the mindset of a panicked woman, on a mission to sell diamond earrings just to make ends meet. And in trying to think from that perspective, Ava started to realize that it wasn't all that impossible to think of a woman in that position being pushed by anger—maybe even pushed hard enough to kill someone she felt had betrayed her.

CHAPTER TWENTY

"Yeah, I'd think this would be the place," Pawlowski said.

And thank God for that, Ava thought. It had been a tiresome task so far, one that she wasn't sure would ever end. Before this little hunt, Ava had never stepped inside a pawn shop, so when she started entering them to ask about a woman selling diamond earrings, she was slightly amazed at the variety of goods. There were clothes, guitars, old jars, books, household items and yes, jewelry. And though Ava had never been the sort of woman that had gone all ga-ga over jewelry, she did have a trained enough eye to tell when something was cheap or of exceptional quality.

By the time they'd visited their fourth pawn shop, Ava wasn't sure it was going to work. They'd asked four different brokers about women selling jewelry and so far their only hit had been an old woman that had sold a rather expensive pocket watch.

"It's strange, actually," that particular broker told them. "With the state of things the way they are, you'd think lots of folks would come in to sell their valuables. But it seems to be the opposite. I don't know if it's because they're hoping things will make a turn for the better really soon or if they're waiting until things get *real* bad."

Ava assumed the broker was leaving out one crucial bit of information, probably so their business seemed more lucrative than it actually was: maybe brokers were a little less inclined to buy expensive items when they knew hardly anyone had money to buy anything.

They'd walked seven blocks when they came to the fifth pawn shop—the one Pawlowski seemed so certain was the right place. Even before they stepped inside, Ava could see that it was the nicest one they'd visited. The windows were clean and polished; some of the nicer items were on display on shelves and little stands: watches, gold chains, collectible coins, rings, and so on.

The interior of the shop proved her right. There was a neat and tidy order to the items displayed around the shop. The lighting was soft and inviting, the air filled with the scent of a cleaning agent of some kind.

They walked up to the counter and were greeted by a jovial man with a thick moustache. As they were the only people in the shop, he seemed more than happy to give them his undivided attention.

"Good morning, ladies," he said. "You looking for anything in particular?"

"You could say that," Ava said, presenting her badge. After identifying themselves, the man behind the counter made a transition from jovial to suddenly very businesslike. "We're trying to track down a woman that recently sold a pair of diamond earrings. Would you happen to remember a woman that fits that description."

"How recently are we talking?"

"Sometime in the past two or three weeks."

"Fortunately for you ladies, not many people have come in selling things like that. So, yes, I do remember a woman that came in. It's been about two weeks, give or take a few days. And actually…"

He paused and looked down beneath the counter he was standing behind. After rummaging around for a few seconds and muttering cheerfully to himself, he stood back up with a small, delicate box in his hands.

"These are the very earrings she sold me. We bickered back and forth on the price a bit, but I think she left mostly happy."

"Do you have a bill of sale, by any chance?" Pawlowski asked.

"I do, indeed. I can fish it out for you, if you'd like."

"That would be amazing," Ava said. "We need to get her address."

"Ah, well then I don't need to go fishing for it at all. When I asked her for an address, she was really mean about it, you know? Like it was none of my business. but I always get at least an address for a customer when it's a transaction of more than twenty-five dollars. She was very rude about it but then finally said she was staying at the Norman Hotel. I remember it because I thought it was odd. She was a pretty lady, you know? Held herself in high regard. You could tell she was…sort of used to people thinking she was the cat's pajamas."

"That's a tremendous help," Pawlowski said. "But just so we can confirm everything, we'd still like you to get that receipt. We'd like to get the woman's name if possible."

"Sure. One second."

The proprietor turned away and walked behind a large case that served as sort of a false wall behind his front counter. He came back thirty seconds later with a single, short slip of paper.

"Right here," he said, handing it over. "K. Branson."

It was the confirmation they needed. It was ironic, in a way, that a pair of earrings sold by the woman in question was going to lead the police to her.

Ava handed the receipt back to the pawn broker, giving him a nod and a smile. "We really do appreciate your help," she said as she and Pawlowski turned back for the exit.

"Any idea where the Norman Hotel is?" Ava asked.

"Yes, actually," Pawlowski said. Her eyes were already scanning the streets for a cab. "I was working with another officer a few weeks ago and busted up a moonshine outfit working out of one of the rooms. It's not exactly an upstanding sort of place. If that *is* where Kathleen Branson ended up, she's taken a very big step down."

Pawlowski waved down a cab and less than three minutes after taking a look at Kathleen Branson's earrings, they were on the way to the Norman Hotel. The cab took them in a mostly direct route but Ava found herself slightly awed and sad at the same time as she realized just how quickly the quality and vibrancy of the city could change. In some places, it really only took a few blocks. It was a feature of the city that had gotten progressively worse the longer the stock market crash continued to gnaw away at everyone and everything.

Not too long after they passed a group of homeless people squatting around the mouth of an alley, the cab driver took a right-hand turn. The tall buildings and overall hum of the city was still present, but it was in a ragged fashion. Ava likened it to a well-trained and athletic boxer that had taken a few too many beatings and now had a hard time breathing and thinking straight.

Several minutes later, the cab pulled into an uneven and slightly dusty parking lot. A boxy-looking building sat just off of the street, looking out onto the city though dingy windows. It wasn't the worst hotel Ava had ever seen, but it was essentially a different world from the apartment complex Branson had been living in up until a few days ago.

They headed directly for the front office. It was a dingy room that was thick with the smell of pipe smoke and dust. A middle-aged man sat behind a cluttered desk, eating a sandwich while thumbing through a stack of papers. When he looked up to greet them, he made no attempt to hide the fact that he was irritated.

"Need a room?" he said, barely looking up at them. But the little glance he did take registered about a second after he returned his attention to the papers. Slowly, he looked back up and, as he looked back and forth between his guests, a small smile began to take shape.

"No thank you," Ava said. She showed her badge and the man looked confused right away. The smile faltered but ultimately remained, though now it looked a bit lopsided. "I'm Detective Ava Gold, NYPD. My partner and I are trying to locate a woman named Kathleen Branson. We have reason to believe she's stayed here at some point in the past several days."

"Branson, you say?"

He seemed happy enough to open up a small ledger that sat at the left edge of the desk. "I don't really pay much attention to the names," he said. "I give them this here ledger and have them sign their name. And…yeah, I got her right here. K. Branson. But I hate to be the one to tell you, she's not here anymore. Checked out last night."

"How long was she here?" Ava asked.

"Two days and nights, looks like. But you know…I did have to get on her and this one other woman. They were being loud and rowdy, sort of arguing a little. And I think…" He stopped, lowered his voice, and leaned forward a little. "…I think the other woman might be one of those women of the night, if you know what I mean."

"What was the argument about?" Pawlowski asked.

"Couldn't tell you. I went out, asked them to break it up, and they did. Not much of a problem."

"Would you happen to know if this other woman is still here?"

"I imagine so. Your Branson woman is the only single woman that checked out today."

"What room number is she in?"

He looked back to the ledger and tapped at a name, smiling at his ability to help. "The only other woman's name that's signed here is Elizabeth Wendell. She's in Room 7."

The entire situation raised several questions in Ava's mind. First of all, how often did single women get rooms at this hotel. Secondly, if the clerk suspected the other woman might be a prostitute, why let her stay? Was there some form of business perk, an assurance that he'd keep his rooms rented out for such activities? She had no time for these questions right now, though. This was the second stop they'd made, only to find that Branson had moved on. And this time, unless the second woman had some sort of information for them, they would have no bread crumbs left to follow.

They thanked the clerk and quickly headed back out to the lot. The rooms were connected by a thin strip of cracked, dingy concrete. On their way to Room 7, they passed by an older man asleep with his back against the walls between Rooms 5 and 6. They literally had to step over his legs to make it by.

Ava knocked on the door and could hear slight movements right away. As she waited, she noticed a slight motion inside the window to the right of the door. Someone had peeked through the thin curtain, peering out. Several seconds later, a woman answered the door. She was rather pretty, with long, curly hair and a figure that looked to have come out of the crude sketches of a sexually charged teenage boy. She wore makeup, though it was clear she'd only been awake for a short while. Her eyes were still bleary with sleep and her hair was a bit messy.

"Yes?" she asked. "Can I help you?"

"We're looking for a woman named Kathleen Branson," Ava said. "We're told the two of you have been spending some time together the last day or so."

"You have, have you?" the woman asked, giving them a curious glance. "And you are?"

"NYPD," Pawlowski said, showing her badge.

"Oh. Well…who told you I know a woman by that name?"

"The gentleman at the front desk," Ava said. "You're Elizabeth Wendell, right?"

"I am. And this woman you're talking about…you're sure she's been here? I haven't spoken to another woman in two or three days. Been here mostly by myself."

A devious little smile crept across her lips after this comment. Ava also noticed that after they'd introduced themselves as the police, Elizabeth Wendell had positioned herself in the center of the doorway, attempting to keep them from entering—or even getting a good view of the room beyond. Noting this, Ava nearly asked her to step aside and let them enter. But before she did, she caught another slight blur of motion. It was all the way to the back of the room, a quick motion slipping into the bathroom—which was just barely still within her sight.

Ava nodded, playing it cool for Wendell while also coming up with a plan that would net the best results.

"You're certain of that?" she asked Wendell.

"Yes, quite."

"Okay. Well, we do understand that Kathleen Branson is in the area. If you hear of anyone by that name being around here, please contact the local police."

"Oh of course," Wendell said. She looked far too eager to oblige, wanting them to leave her alone. "Anything else?"

"No, that's it. Thanks very much."

As Wendell closed the door, Ava stepped back and instantly noticed Pawlowski's look of confusion. "What the hell?" she asked. "We can't just let her—"

"Head to the back," Ava said, interrupting. "Someone was moving around quickly in the bathroom. If there's a window back there, maybe they're trying to get out of it. I'll stay here in case anyone tries sneaking out of the door."

Pawlowski's eyes lit up with excitement. She nodded and raced to the left, quickly rounding the corner of the motel. When she was gone, Ava pressed herself lightly against the side of the building, positioned directly between Elizabeth Wendell's door and window. She readied herself, her ankles and calves ready to spring into action if the door opened up. Of course, she knew there was no guarantee that the movement she'd seen had been Kathleen, but it *had* seemed as if Wendell had been doing her best to block the sight of the room. And the motion hadn't occurred until after Ava had made it clear that they needed to speak with Kathleen Branson.

As it turned out, though, Ava didn't have much time to doubt her instincts. It took less than ten seconds before she heard Pawlowski cry out from behind the building.

"Gold! She's out! She's out and she's on the move!"

Ava pushed herself from the side of the building and ran in the same direction Pawlowski had gone just moments before. And when she came around the back of the building to see Pawlowski giving chase, she found that if this woman was indeed Kathleen Branson, she was incredibly fast—and she apparently wasn't going to go down easily.

CHAPTER TWENTY ONE

It was hard for Ava to tell if the woman—who she assumed was indeed Kathleen Branson—was very strategic or had no idea where she was going. When she ran away from the Norman Hotel, she took an almost immediate left down an alleyway that was hidden by a small, ramshackle building and a construction site. She cut through the construction site, which Ava thought was a smart move because it presented both Ava and Pawlowski with numerous unpredictable obstacles. By the angle she was headed, Ava assumed the woman was going for the newly installed subway on this side of the city, but she ended up veering west of that location.

She supposed it didn't matter where she was headed. She was running—and as far as Ava was concerned, that was an indication of guilt. Not only that, but she was running *fast*. Ava had managed to catch up with Pawlowski, trailing her by about three paces. But Kathleen was easily half a block ahead of them by the time Ava and Pawlowski had cleared the construction site.

For a blinding moment when the world seemed to be nothing more than a blur of motion around them, Ava felt almost dizzy. The tall and still-growing part of Manhattan loomed large ahead of them, the towering buildings like some strange and exotic animal, welcoming them into its folds so it could devour them. Ava loved her city, specifically Manhattan, but she did sometimes feel that it was growing too quickly. It was a feeling that was reinforced as she and Pawlowski did their best to chase down Kathleen Branson.

Branson was heading toward Morningside Park, but Ava was starting to think she may not make it. She'd started running too hard too soon and it was clear that she wasn't used to such strenuous activities. And while even Pawlowski seemed to be slowing a bit and growing winded, Ava had managed to keep her breathing calm and collected. It came from some of the stamina training she'd done with her father in the boxing gym, making sure you never got winded by the time the third round came along.

As Ava slowly overlook Pawlowski, she could easily tell that Kathleen was getting tired. Not only was she slowing down, but she was hunching forward slightly as she continued to draw in huge, gasping breaths.

"Stop running!" Ava called out. "You're only making it harder on yourself, Ms. Branson."

Kathleen continued to sprint on, but just for a few more strides. She glanced over her shoulder, saw how much faster Ava was covering her same ground, and then hit her knees. She did so on the sidewalk in front of a small delicatessen about half a block away from Morningside Park. There were only a few people milling around on the streets, all looking at the fallen woman and the two others that were rushing toward her. Ava noticed that a few men were grinning at the situation, as if wondering what these three daffy dames were up to.

Only one man on the street seemed to have any real heart to him. Having seen Kathleen fall to her knees, he removed his hat in a chivalrous gesture and approached her. He was speaking softly to her when Ava approached. He took up an almost defensive posture as Ava came in fast and aggressive.

"What's the meaning of th—" he started.

"New York Police Department," Ava said, angling in toward Kathleen. "Move aside, sir."

"Oh, I don't think so. You expect me to believe that you—"

Pawlowski filled the distance, taking the last few strides to join with Ava. She wasn't having any of this man's interruptions. She flashed her badge at him and, for a moment, Ava thought she might actually shove him.

"Out of the way, you stupid lug! NYPD!"

It wasn't so much the sight of the badge, but also the tone of Pawlowski's voice that caused the man to take two large steps back. If there was any remaining hesitancy in him, it vanished when Ava pulled out her cuffs. Satisfied that he'd seen enough and knew he wasn't needed, Ava was finally able to ignore him.

She began to apply the cuffs, but Kathleen still had some fight remaining. "Oh, for God's sake, is that really necessary?" she asked as she tried to struggle away.

It was the first solid glimpse she'd gotten of Kathleen during the entire chase. She was small with bobbing blonde hair. She was pretty in a plain sort of way, but her lips were the true star of the show. They were luscious and plump, the sort most men would stare at as they spoke with her as opposed to her eyes. As for her eyes, they were currently fuming with anger, the blue of them almost stormy.

"When you make us chase on you on foot for nearly half a mile, yes, it is," Ava said.

"Doesn't help that you escaped through a bathroom window, either," Pawlowski added.

"Well, what the hell is this about anyway?" Kathleen asked.

With the cuffs already slapped around the woman's wrists and locked, Av asked: "Is your name Kathleen Branson?"

"It is."

"Then we'd like to speak with you," Ava said. "And before you tried running off on us, the questions would have likely been fairly easy."

"Well, I can tell you this: I've done nothing as to need cuffing…and out in public, of all things!"

Ava helped the woman to her feet and was fully prepared to flag down a cab to take Branson back to the office. But just before she could start looking, Pawlowski stepped up directly beside her and whispered into her ear.

"We shouldn't take her back unless we know for absolutely certain she knows something that can help with the case. We take her in and she's innocent all around, Captain Miller will close this thing right away."

Ava knew that she was right. She'd gotten so caught up and overcome with energy and adrenaline from the footrace that she hadn't even thought of that. She glanced around and saw a small bench sitting in front of one of the entrances to Morningside Park. There were a few people passing by, in the process of visits or daily errands, but nothing too busy. And in this part of the city, it wasn't as if they were going to find a quiet, private place anyway.

"We're going to head over to that bench," Ava said. "Once we're seated, I'll remove the cuffs. If you try to run again, I'll simply catch you again and then you *will* go to jail for a few days. Understood?"

"Yes! Just get me out of these damned cuffs!"

As Ava and Pawlowski escorted Kathleen across the street to the bench, Ava thought she understood why being handcuffed was such a trigger for Kathleen. If her hunch was correct, Kathleen had enjoyed having a man pamper her with money and extravagances. To go from that to having to live in a place like the Norman Hotel must be humiliating. Getting handcuffed in public probably felt like a cheap shot, the final kick to the head while she was already down.

The three women made it across the street and sat down on the bench, with Kathleen between both officers. Ava did her best to seem somewhat subtle about unlocking the cuffs. When Kathleen's arms were free, she brought them to her lap and started massaging them. She made no attempt to run though; she was still trying to catch her breath from the chase.

"I'm going to ask you a series of questions," Ava said, "and after those questions, I'm going to need you to tell me why you ran when you heard there were police looking for you."

"Oh, I can tell you that right now. It's embarrassing, but not worth getting in more trouble over. Two nights ago, I left a hotel without paying. Is that what this is about? Was that worth the run-down?"

"That is *not* what this about," Ava said. "We need to ask you some questions about a man named Alfred Perkins." She waited a moment to read Kathleen's face. The woman's expression told her all she needed to know. There was a flash of anger, followed by a residual disappointment that settled on her face in the form of a frown.

"Looks like the name rings a bell," Pawlowski said.

"Tell us how you know him," Ava ordered.

"Just a guy…you know? We fancied each other and were sort of dating."

"Did you know he was married?"

Kathleen nodded. She looked slightly ashamed for a moment but then did her best to try holding her head up high. "And we honestly didn't…well, you know…we didn't do anything that often. Just slept together a few times, and he really did neat himself up over it. I think it's why he…"

"Do you think it's why he was funneling money to you?" Ava asked. "Do you feel like his guilt over what he was doing caused him to pay you money?"

"Sometimes, yes. I'll admit it. But Alfred is just…he's a kind, giving person, anyway. The sort of man that likes to give gifts."

"But he stopped giving you money, right?" Ava asked. "We've been to the apartment you were staying in. The landlord says you got out of there…that he kicked you out."

"He did…and yes, it was because I couldn't afford it without Alfred helping. I don't even know where he is now. I assume he's still working at that job even though he's told me time and time again that the market is just pitiful. He had to make cuts here and there. He told me the last time I saw him that in a few weeks, he'd barely even be able to pay his own bills or take care of his wife."

"So he had to make a choice," Pawlowski said.

"Yes."

"One thing, though," Ava said. "You just told us that you don't know where he is right now…or what he's up to. When was the last time you saw him?"

Kathleen took a moment to think about it, looking down to her wrists as she continued to rub at them. "Two weeks? Maybe closer to three. He came by the apartment just to check on me. He…well, I was so mad at him because he'd promised I'd never want for anything. He really did feel bad there just before I called it off."

"So you ended things with him?" Ava asked.

"Yeah. I'm not a heartless wretch, you know. I didn't want him to abandon his wife. I mean, I wouldn't have argued if that's the choice he made, but I understood it. And when he left that last time, I knew that was it. And now…well, here I am. You saw where I was staying. I was having to share a room with Elizabeth because neither of us could afford our own." She shrugged and added: "The clerk didn't know, though."

Ava wasn't sure if she bought the story. It didn't *seem* like she was lying, but Ava knew how dangerous it could be to trust a person at their word.

"Kathleen, where were you two nights ago?"

"At that same lousy hotel. I was with Elizabeth for a bit, but I had my own room that night. It's a good thing, too, because she was…well, she was *working* in her room."

"Did anyone else see you around the hotel that night?" Pawlowski asked.

"I suppose. The clerk was there, and I spoke with him for a while. And when Elizabeth was done, I hung out with her. I also visited a friend of mine a little later on, a broad that owes me some money from a while back."

"You're being honest with us?" Ava asked. "If we go back and ask the clerk about this…?"

"Yes, I'm telling the truth. What are you even…hold on. Wait. What is it? What's happened?"

Ava knew it would never be enough to convince a jury, but the flash of worry she saw come across Kathleen's face told her everything. Up until this very moment, Kathleen Branson had no idea that Alfred Perkins had died.

Pawlowski seemed to be take note of this, too, because when she spoke again her voice was soft and somber. "Ms. Branson, have you ever spent any time near the site of the Chrysler Building?"

The question seemed to legitimately confuse Kathleen. She looked back and forth between Ava and Pawlowski as if she were expecting either of them to finish a joke at any moment,

"No. I've passed by it a few times since they started building it, but…no. Please tell me what's going on. Has something happened to Alfred?"

She had a glistening of tears in her eyes already and when Ava broke the news to her, they spilled freely. Ava did not approve of the relationship that Kathleen and Alfred had shared, but she also knew a broken heart was a broken heart no matter how you looked at it. She hated to have broken the news in such a way and, more than that, felt almost guilty that her mind had already moved on to other aspects of the case.

Kathleen Branson was not their killer. Which meant they were back to having no leads and very likely less than a day to find the truth. Ava sat with a weeping Kathleen Branson and Pawlowski (whom Ava was learning was very uncomfortable with the sight of someone crying), trying to think of which step to take next.

CHAPTER TWENTY TWO

"So what are we supposed to do now?" Pawlowski asked.

They'd left Kathleen ten minutes ago. She'd still been crying when they left but insisted that she'd be okay. She'd go back to Elizabeth's room and figure out what she could do from here on out. Ava felt for the woman but also figured she had, in a way, done it to herself in allowing a man to pay for every single expenditure without having that same man as her husband.

"I honestly don't know," Ava answered. They'd not yet hailed a cab, simply walking in the direction of the precinct, which was still roughly four miles away. "For me, the answer is usually going back to the crime scene or digging through records and reports. But we've pretty much exhausted revisiting the crime scene, and there aren't really any records to dig into. What about you, Pawlowski? Any ideas?"

"I have one, but I don't think you're going to like it."

"Well, let's hear it anyway."

"I think we just need to go back to the precinct and face the music, as they say. No sense in thinking we're running against the clock without actually being told that's the case."

Ava knew it was the best way to look at things, but it also felt like defeat. She was pretty sure that Frank would have been suggesting the same thing, reminding her that sometimes the face a crime presents is its actual face—that there isn't always an alternative answer. And in this case, maybe the glaring, obvious answer was that Alfred Perkins *had* killed himself.

"I hate to say it, but I think you might be right."

Her agreement brought on a silence that lingered between them, awkward and uneasy. For the first time, Ava found herself wishing she'd never been sent to the Seventeenth Precinct. She understood that change was good and she even understood the reasoning behind Minard's decision (along with the Chief) to move her. She also knew that if she'd been given this case at the old precinct, with Frank as her partner, she'd be facing the exact same hiccups and obstacles. In that moment, though, she just missed the familiarity of it all.

She began to scan the streets for a cab, but saw none. She knew there would be more of them several blocks further ahead as they neared the busier part of Manhattan. And that was fine with her. Some time spent walking might help her to clear her head, to help to—

Up ahead, she saw a familiar face in a thin stream of pedestrians on the sidewalk. She stopped walking as her head and heart tried to process what they were seeing.

Not quite a block away, Frank was standing by a man in a nice trench coat, speaking rather quietly about something. This obviously made no sense because he had no business being on their side of town. She tried to recall any case they'd worked on that had brought them this far out but couldn't think of anything.

In that moment, she forgot that she was walking with Pawlowski. She started walking faster, her eyes now locked on Frank. She was ecstatic to see him but was also curious as to what might have brought him all the way out here. Before she was aware she was doing it, Ava was sprinting towards him. As she did, she watched as Frank nodded politely to the man he'd been speaking to, breaking the conversation, and then turning around. He started walking in the opposite direction, further away from Ava. She watched as he took a right at the end of the block, walking out of her sight.

She could hear Pawlowski calling out behind her, but she was far too focused to turn around to address her. With Frank out of her sight, there was no guarantee she'd be able to find him now. She knew perhaps better than anyone just how easily it was to lose sight of someone in the unpredictable flow of New York City's pedestrian traffic.

"Gold, what are you doing?"

But Ava pressed on, coming to the same corner she'd watched Frank go around just fifteen seconds earlier. When she rounded the corner, she was relieved to see that there weren't many people on the street. She caught sight of Frank right away, just several feet ahead of her. He was walking slowly, looking down at a newspaper in his hands and—

Ava's heart plummeted.

It wasn't Frank at all. It was a man that bore a slight resemblance to Frank but now that she was up close, the differences were very clear to see. This man was a bit shorter, and his hair was not only darker, but longer.

A wave of embarrassment washed over her. She stood in place, not sure if she wanted to be angry or sad. She watched the man walk on, nodding to a few people that passed by him. Ava's heart still ached a bit as she started to understand just how upset she truly was about how Frank had basically distanced himself from her ever since the meeting in Minard's office two days ago. She'd tried to convince herself it wasn't too big of a deal, but that denial was quickly wearing off.

"Detective Gold?"

She turned at the sound of Pawlowski's voice, still feeling embarrassed. "Sorry about that," she said.

"Is everything okay?"

"Yes, I just saw someone…or I thought I saw someone I knew. But I was wrong."

Pawlowski nodded, looking over Ava's shoulder at the handful of people moving about the sidewalk. "But you're okay? You're sure? You looked like you saw a ghost or something there for a second."

"Yes, I'm fine."

But that was far from the truth. Something about thinking she'd seen Frank had stirred something in her. While she knew it wasn't an absolutely certainty that this case would be officially closed if they went back to the precinct and spoke with Miller, she felt like there was a very good chance. And as far as she was concerned, there were far too many open ends and coincidences in this case for her to comfortably make the assumption that Alfred Perkins had killed himself.

And deeper down, where honesty sometimes hid away out of fear of being ignored, there was another truth: she didn't want Frank to think she'd be a failure without him.

What haven't we done? she thought. *What steps have we not covered?*

The answer came to her easily enough but she was pretty sure it, too, would turn out to be a dead end.

"What?" Pawlowski asked. "What is it?"

"Let's wait to head back to the precinct. I think there's another stop we need to make."

"Gold, I am *not* climbing those stairs at the Chrysler Building again."

"No, not the Chrysler Building. We never bothered going to the coroner. And as far as I could tell from the initial report, neither did anyone else."

"At the risk of sounding cruel, I'm not sure there's any point," Pawlowski said. "I'd imagine that after a fall from that height, there wouldn't be much of a body to look over."

"And you might be right. But I have to make sure we've checked everything before we go back to the precinct with our tails between our legs."

Pawlowski considered it for a moment, going so far as to rub at her forehead as if trying her best to push away an oncoming headache. "My God, Gold. You don't like to lose, do you?"

"I don't. But it's more than that. It's…"

She wasn't sure how to explain it. It came down to justice, she supposed. Even if they kept pushing and found at the end of the day that Perkins *had* killed himself, at least then she'd *know*. She could rest comfortably knowing she'd tried everything she could to prove otherwise. But as the case currently stood, that was not a position she was ready to take.

"I know," Pawlowski said. "We have to at least try. But…you know not to expect much, right?"

"Right."

Ava glanced back at the man she'd mistaken for Frank. He was at the end of the block now, starting to cross the street. And as she watched him, she saw an approaching cab. She stepped to the edge of the street and began to flag it down, suddenly very anxious to get to their next stop along the course of this case.

CHAPTER TWENTY THREE

Ava had fully expected to visit the coroner's office and have them tell her that there was simply nothing to pull any sort of evidence from. What she hadn't expected was the look of utter bewilderment from the coroner. After telling him why they were there, the coroner looked at her with an expression a child might give an adult if they'd been asked why they liked sweets.

"You're really asking me if there was any evidence on the body?"

The coroner was a middle-aged man with a completely bald head. He was also rather tall, so when he gave his perplexed look, he did it in a way that made it appear as if he was looking down on Ava and Pawlowski.

"Yes, anything at all," Ava said.

They were sitting in his office, a cluttered and very small room. Ava wasn't sure, but she thought Pawlowski seemed relieved to know that they wouldn't be looking at any examination tables.

"There was nothing," the coroner said. "Now, I did end up removing a few items from the body, mind you: fragments of glass, a small piece of metal from the hood of the car he slammed into. The body itself, though, has been delivered to a university upstate. They're wanting to study the skeleton in order to get a better glimpse at how the spine responds to such a fall." He shook his head, frowned, and added: "Though I don't know that they're going to be able to tell much of anything."

"That bad?" Pawlowski asked.

The coroner chuckled a bit. "Yes, you could say that. Ladies…a fall from that height is particularly nasty. I've only ever seen one before it—a construction worker that fell to his death over at the Empire State Building site. In the case of Mr. Perkins, his spine had pretty much been obliterated. His ribs, the same—with the exception of two ribs on his left side, which had blasted right through his skin. His hip had popped out of socket on both sides and had been twisted nearly one hundred and eighty degrees. I was told that removing his body from that car took nearly fifteen minutes." He sighed and shook his head.

"So now do you understand why I find it foolish to think there would have been anything in terms of evidence?"

It was indeed a grisly depiction, but Ava also didn't think he'd be speaking so snidely to two male officers that were sitting across his desk. Still, she'd already learned that lesson multiple times, and she wasn't about to anger what might be the one last person to keep this case from being closed.

"There was no weapon on him?" Ava asked.

"Not that I'm aware of. But that's usually handled by your people, right?"

"Right," she said, really starting to become unnerved by his condescending tone.

"Look, if you're searching for something that would indicate he was perhaps pushed or thrown from that height, I'm just afraid there is nothing to support it. But here's what I will do. I'll bring you the things I removed from him…the glass, the metal, some grime I removed from his tongue. You can have a look at it all but after that, I'm afraid there's really nothing I can do to assist you with this."

Before Ava could even thank him, the coroner was up and exiting his office, leaving Ava and Pawlowski sitting by themselves.

"Gold, this is starting to seem a little crazy," Pawlowski said. "Honestly, maybe even a little creepy. You heard the man…there was nothing left of the body."

"Well, we're here now. Might as well see it through, right?"

Pawlowski said nothing. She simply looked away, her eyes trailing to her hands and studying her fingernails. It then occurred to Ava that Pawlowski may have never gone to these lengths before. For all she knew, she'd never had to step foot in a coroner's office. After all, Ava knew next to nothing about her partner's career.

"Pawlowski…is this all new to you?" she asked.

"What do you mean?"

"Tracking down leads like this. Having to visit a coroner in the hopes of finding a scrap of evidence."

There was a brief moment where Pawlowski looked insulted, but it passed quickly as she nodded. "I mean, I've been on investigative cases in the past. But I've never actually run after someone like we ran after Kathleen Branson. And this is the first time I've had to come to a coroner's office."

Ava hated that Pawlowski seemed embarrassed by this admission, so she carried the conversation on as naturally as she could. "Sorry if

I've pushed you too far. I didn't even stop to think…to ask you what you were comfortable with."

"Oh, there's no need to be sorry. I don't want Miller to shut this down, either. I've had more excitement in these past two days than the past two *months*."

It did seem odd to Ava that Miller had paired them up. Sure, there was some obvious marketing and public image to the idea of two women officers working together. But it also almost felt as if they were being set up to fail all at the same time. Something about the idea snagged at the corners of her mind but none of it had time to develop. Behind them, the coroner came back into the office. He was carrying a small, metal tray which he sat on his desk directly in front of Ava and Pawlowski.

"As I said, it's not much." He returned to his seat and watched them both as they leaned in toward the tray. Ava could feel his eyes on them, the weight of his stare essentially telling them to make this as quick as possible so he could get back to work and not waste his time with a man that clearly jumped to his death on purpose.

Ava ignored his glare and looked at the meager collection of items taken from the body of Alfred Perkins. There were two keys, presumably taken from his pockets. She also saw the glass and four small fragments of metal from the car. There was also a small bit of cloth which was tucked into a plastic bag; the grime the coroner had indicated had come from Perkins's tongue was on it. She didn't think much of it because it really looked like nothing more than dust or dirt. And surely, falling from such a height had knocked up some dirt.

The final item, though, caught Ava's attention. It was small and seemingly inconsequential at first glance—a piece of fabric, torn ragged at the edges. The piece of fabric was not large at all. She estimated it to be about four inches long by an inch and a half wide. It looked to be silk but as she leaned in closer, she saw that it was a cheap knock-off, a type of fabric that had been thinned out and manufactured to *look* like silk. It was blue in color, with a lazy gray stitching pattern in the shape of intertwined diamonds.

"This was on his body?" Ava asked, pointing to the piece of fabric.

"Yes. It was trapped between his middle and ring fingers. I believe he was likely clutching it as he fell, but it shifted in his fall and was lodged between his fingers."

"Do you recall what he was wearing?"

"A suit. But the undershirt had been pretty much destroyed."

"So nothing with this fabric, with this pattern?"

"No."

"And…wait. You mean to tell me this was *in his hand* and wasn't deemed important enough to be viewed as a piece of evidence?"

The coroner bristled a bit at her tone and she could see from the caution in his eyes that at least a small part of him knew that she was right to be upset. "Be realistic," he said. "Given the state of things around the city and the unrest everywhere, this looks like a suicide from every possible angle you can view it. Surely you see that."

She did. She *had*…for the entirety of this case; she knew what it looked like. But she'd felt like it was her job to find a new angle. And looking at that scrap of fabric, she was quite sure she had indeed found one.

"Seeing as how you've accepted this as a suicide," Ava said, "I'm assuming you wouldn't mind if I took this scrap of fabric."

The coroner raised his hands in mock defeat and smiled. "You're the police. Do whatever you want."

"Oh, if only," she muttered as she picked up the piece of fabric. "Thank you for your time."

She got up and left quickly, not understanding just how much his attitude had bothered her until she was out of the office. Pawlowski caught up with her as she came to the end of the hallway.

"What was that?" Pawlowski asked. "Did you piece something together?"

"Maybe. But more than that, the whole approach to this man's death has seemed lazy. Yes, I understand it looks like a suicide. But it took you and I all of…what? Maybe three hours to find at least one moving piece that suggested there might be something else to it?"

Pawlowski nodded her understanding. "So the fabric…do you have any ideas?"

"I do. And on the way to maybe get some answers, I guess you'll get a quick history lesson on Ava Gold."

Smiling as she held the door open for Ava, Pawlowski said: "Sounds like fun."

They stepped back out into the street and started looking for another cab. Ava fingered the fabric in her pocket, knowing that what she had in mind might be a long shot. But she had to at least try. It was now 12:10, and they were quickly running out of time.

CHAPTER TWENTY FOUR

"For a period of about two years, I was pretty deep into the local jazz scene," Ava said.

"What?" Pawlowski asked, seemingly astounded. "You?"

"Yes. And while it might seem like I'm bragging, I had started to get popular with some of the local bands. I'd get calls from clubs to lead certain groups here and there."

"You? Jazz?" Pawlowski chuckled, apparently unable to see it.

They were in the back of a cab, the driver taking them a bit out of their original way, in the direction of Harlem.

"Yes. Me."

"But hold on. I'd heard you used to screw around at a boxing gym…that you were pretty good in the ring."

"Yeah, I did that, too. When your father is a fairly well-known boxer, it sort of comes with the territory."

"Jazz singer. Boxer. Detective. Ava Gold, you're one mixed-up dame, you know that?"

"So I've been told. Anyway, as you might imagine, being somewhat familiar with the jazz scene has given me certain connections. Here and there, those connections have come in handy when I needed information about seedier places and characters in regard to cases."

"Okay. So are you telling me you've got some sort of connection that is going to have answers about how Alfred Perkins was killed?"

"Nothing that direct, no. But this," she said, taking the piece of fabric out of her pocket, "does sort of lead me in that direction."

"Yeah, what is it, anyway? Silk?"

"No, it's some sort of fake silk. I mean, you can even feel it and know it's not the real thing. I could spot it pretty easily because there are a lot of singers on the jazz circuit that wear it. From a distance, it looks like the real deal and gives you that glamorous look. And based on the simple, but elegant stitching design, it looks like it might have come from a man's shirt. Like right along the lapel, maybe."

"Okay…"

"If you recall, one of the people on that list we took from Perkins's office was a guy named Isaac O'Hare. I thought I'd heard the name before when I saw it, but seeing this fabric at the coroner's office brought it all back to me."

"Brought what back to you?"

"O'Hare used to work with small tailors in the area to create dresses and gowns for jazz singers. He made shirts for the men, too, but they were really too expensive for jazz musicians to wear. If you're in a jazz band, it's really the singer—the one that's up front and center—that gets the nicer look."

"Why would Perkins have the name of a fabric manufacturer on his list? Seems a little small-time, doesn't it?"

"Well, O'Hare had a larger network behind him, I think. I obviously never looked deep into it because why would I? I was just interested in the clothes. But I'm fairly certain he had a textile mill, or was running one cooperatively with a partner. I just don't know."

"And that's the address you gave the driver just now?" Pawlowski asked.

"Yes. I wasn't sure of the *exact* location, but it'll be close. I only ever picked up stuff from his little shop—and that was only a grand total of two times."

They fell silent for a moment, both considering the many possibilities. If O'Hare had truly been one of Perkins's clients, had the crash hit him as badly as so many others? And if so, what sort of money had he lost?

And the bigger question, one she wasn't quite ready to speak out loud: *Had this piece of fabric somehow come from O'Hare just before Perkins fell to his death?*

It took another twelve minutes before the cab finally arrived at the destination. It turned out that Ava's memory was better than she'd hoped. When they stepped out of the car, she saw O'Hare's shop nestled between an abandoned building and what looked to be a struggling leather manufacturer. She noted the very small number of people on the streets, denoting just how dead this part of the city had become. She was sure that if they traveled deeper into Harlem, it would get even worse.

As she started for the shop, she heard Pawlowski behind her, asking the cab driver to please stay there for a moment. They then approached the door together but even before they tried the door, Ava could tell the place was closed. There was no sign indicating that the proprietor was out and would be back soon. There wasn't even a sign that some shop owners used to indicated if they were open or closed. Ava looked in through the small window and saw an empty counter. There were a few fabric racks along the back walls that were mostly empty. The place looked utterly deserted, and she wondered how long it had been in this state.

"Any idea where the textile mill is?" Pawlowski asked.

"No, but I'm pretty certain it's nearby. We could have the driver circle around a few blocks and see if we get lucky."

Pawlowski nodded and they walked back to the cab. As they did, it occurred to Ava that she had some other options at her disposal if things became too difficult. They could find a phone and call the precinct, hoping to get an address for the mill. Or if Pawlowski thought they shouldn't contact anyone at the Seventeenth Precinct, Ava could place a call to her old offices. Maybe she could ask for Frank. And if he was out on the streets, Frances or Lottie down in the basement that served as the Women's Division would be happy to help.

Thinking of the women she'd first worked with when coming to the job made her realize just how far she'd come. She was sad that her promotion to detective and assignment to partner with Frank had turned her away from them but it was also encouraging to know that she'd consistently done good work and had kept her mantle of detective.

These thoughts were brought to a halt when, just five minutes later, the cab driver took a right and pointed the car into a dusty-looking section of Harlem. A vacant, dirty car park was located to the right and then, directly beside that, a small warehouse. It looked familiar enough for Ava to think it might be worth looking at.

"Stop here, please," Ava told the driver, pointing to the curb in front of the mill.

He did, and Ava and Pawlowski stepped out of the car. They made their way to the front door, a large wooden relic that showed clear signs of age and abuse. Despite its weakened appearance, it was locked and seemed just as sturdy as the rest of the building. However, there was a small wooden sign hanging a little off of center that told them they had found the right place. It read: O'HARE TEXTILES. And then, it small print beneath it: *If door is locked, come to loading door on the side.*

Ava and Pawlowski followed these instructions. The loading door faced the vacant lot they'd seen when the cab had turned onto this particular street. Yet when they got to the loading door, they found it just as inaccessible as the front door. The clasp at the bottom of the door—which was much larger than the front door—was held in place by a bolt and a simple lock that was drilled into a concrete slab at the very end of the walkway they were standing on.

"Well, this seems pointless," Pawlowski said.

"That's the spirit."

Pawlowski opened her mouth to respond when they heard a slight cry from inside. It wasn't a cry of pain but more like one of distress or frustration. And as far as Ava was concerned, it was more than enough reason to force their way in.

"I'm pretty sure we could break that," Ava said, looking to the lock.

"Is that a good idea, though?" Pawlowski asked.

Ava shrugged as she scanned the lot behind them and it didn't take long for her to spot a few old, crumbled pieces of cement. It was discarded material, maybe from a clean-up crew that had been on the empty lot. She walked back down to the lot, grabbed a chunk of the old concrete that was roughly the size of a melon, and went back to the door.

"Want me to do it?" Pawlowski asked. "If one of us gets in trouble, maybe it should be m—"

Ava kneeled down, drew the chunk of concrete up, and brought it down on the lock with as much force as she could muster. The lock was apparently just as old as the building because the clasp shattered like glass. She tossed the chunk of concrete—also now cracked and a bit broken—aside.

"Well, never mind then," Pawlowski said.

Ava removed the lock and as she pushed the pieces to the side, Pawlowski grabbed the door's large, metal handle. She pulled it open, revealing a musty interior. Ava noticed at once that there were no lights on. There were countless tables and workstations defined by rows of counters, but that was all. As they stepped inside, Ava noticed a few stacks of wooden crates near the back of the building, pushed into a far corner. Other than that and a few scattered remnants of cloth and fabric, the place was empty. She thought she could smell fabric in the air, though, the ghost of what the place had been once upon a time.

"Over there," Pawlowski said, pointing to the far wall and near the front of the building. "Is that an office?"

Ava spotted the little section that was walled off, looking out onto the work floor through a single dingy window. It was clear there was no one in the building, but she wondered if there might have been some paperwork left behind—receipts, banks statements, anything that might potentially link the business back to Alfred Perkins. She knew it was a very long shot, but she figured it was worth looking into as long as they were here.

They made their way across the empty textile mill, their footfalls echoing. It was hard to get an accurate guess as to how long the place had been shut down. Ava guessed it likely hadn't been more than a few weeks just because of the lingering smell of fabric and machine oil in the air.

They came to the office and found the door partially open. Ava reached out to push it open, and was then stopped by a voice from inside.

"Whoever's out there, I have a gun," a man's voice said. "Might as well leave now anyway because there's nothing here to steal."

Ava took a single step back, quietly drawing her sidearm. She looked back to Pawlowski and saw that she was doing the same. Looking to the door, Ava said: "I'm with NYPD and I have a gun, too." She made a point not to mention the fact that she also had a partner with her. She figured it would give her the upper hand if the armed man was taken by surprise by a second intruder.

"But you're a dame," the voice responded.

"There's no fooling you, huh?" Ava said. "I'm going to open this door. Can you put the gun down?"

Several seconds passed before she got a response. "I've lowered it to the floor, but I'm not letting it go."

Ava didn't even give him a second to spare, to rethink his answer. She pushed the door open with her right hand, giving Pawlowski a *stay-put* gesture with her left. When she stepped inside, she saw a man sitting behind a desk. The desk was cluttered with a few boxes, loose sheets of papers, and several old scraps of fabric. The man sitting behind the desk was a bit on the older side, maybe knocking on the door of sixty. He had thin, wiry black hair and a gaunt face. His hollow-looking eyes stared directly at Ava's face. She also noticed that his right arm was hanging down below the desk, out of sight.

"What's your name, sir?" Ava asked. She held her own gun low as well, making sure he knew she did not see him as a threat—yet.

"How about you tell me why the police are here?" he argued. "Actually, why don't you tell me why the police saw fit to break into my work? I assume you busted past the lock on the loading door?"

"We did. And we're here because we're trying to put the pieces together concerning a death that is going to be ruled a suicide unless we can find differently."

"So you've come to a closed-down textile mill? Doesn't make a lot of sense."

"What's your name, sir?"

"Isaac O'Hare."

"That's fortunate," Ava said. "As it turns out, you're exactly the man I need to speak to."

"Is that so?" He grinned and sat forward just a bit. Ava tensed up, ready to bring her gun up if necessary. She still sensed no immediate threat from O'Hare, but she sensed something sightly unhinged about him. "And why is that?"

"Because your name was on a small list we found in the office of the recently departed. What was your relationship with Alfred Perkins?"

"Perkins? What has he d—"

But he stopped, likely understanding fully what was meant. He considered this for a moment and then surprised Ava by letting out a small laugh. "He's the one you're looking into? Well, let me save you the trouble. I find it very likely that Alfred Perkins killed himself."

"And why do you say that?"

"Because he had people like me mad at him." he sat forward again, moving quickly this time, and Ava brought her gun up a bit. O'Hare noticed this and did his best to relax. "Take this very mill, for example. That man lost eighty-five percent of the money I had tied into it. It was just...*all gone.* Sure, he blamed it on the crash, but I know why the crash happened in the first place. Men like him, looking out for themselves and not giving a damn about the people out here that make a living by the sweat of their brows. So because of people like him, I'm out of a job and a building very soon. Not to mention the sixteen people I had working here. They now don't have jobs, either."

Ava used her free hand to reach into her pocket, removing the piece of fabric the coroner had given them. "This scrap of fabric was on Perkins. I seem to recall you once selling fabrics just like these to jazz singers. If you can—"

O'Hare moved so quickly that Ava almost fired by impulse alone. He stood to his feet and pointed his gun at her. It was so sudden and unexpected that Ava didn't understand the inherent danger of the moment until she sensed Pawlowski stepping into the doorway behind her.

"That seems a little unnecessary," Pawlowski said. "Put the gun down, Mr. O'Hare."

"You're here to question me about…what? About *murdering* someone?"

"Yes," Ava said. "And I'm starting to believe we were on to something, given how easily you pulled that gun on me just now. Drop it, O'Hare. It's two on one and so far, we can maybe sweep this under the rug if you'll just cooperate."

"Cooperate," he said, chuckling again. "You bring a piece of fabric in here, accusing me of having some sort of link with Perkins? What the hell am I supposed to think?"

"Mr. O'Hare, you're clearly getting worked up. I really need you to put that gun down before you do something you'll regret."

This time he laughed uproariously, and Ava was now certain that he was not in his right mind. "Well, I've attempted to shoot myself with it. Put it in my mouth and everything, but just couldn't bring myself to do it. I couldn't…."

Ava felt Pawlowski coming in closer, felt her inching toward O'Hare. She came beside Ava and then continued forward. She'd placed her hands down by her hips, making a show of holstering her gun. She then raised her hands and lowered her voice, speaking as sweetly as a princess—a tone Ava had not yet heard from her.

"Mr. O'Hare, you aren't the first person we've spoken to during this case that has lost everything because of the financial ruin this city is going through. But if you would just lower than gun, put in on your desk, and just give us five minutes of your time, it would be a huge help."

It was a masterful performance. Ava watched the hostility drain right out of O'Hare's face. Watching Pawlowski at work, she couldn't help but wonder if she, Ava, had been so worried about trying to appear strong-willed and tough in a male-dominated profession that she'd overlooked the many benefits the soft, sweet side of a woman could offer.

O'Hare didn't lower his gun all the way, but he did lower it to where the barrel was angled towards the floor.

"That's good, Mr. O' Hare," Pawlowski said. "That's really—"

Pawlowski interrupted herself by reaching out and grabbing the arm that held the gun. O'Hare shrieked in surprise and then out of pain as

Pawlowski wrenched his wrist hard to the right. He released the pistol and it fell to the ground with a clatter. Ava sprang forward next and helped with the assist. She took O'Hare's other arm and though he did his best to fight, they were able to bring both arms behind his back and cuff him.

This pair of cuffs is getting quite the workout today, Ava thought.

For a moment, Ava thought O'Hare was crying as she made sure he stood up straight. But after a few seconds, it was clear that he was laughing. She wasn't quite sure about what, but she did know that he'd just held a gun on two officers and had admitted to losing everything because of Alfred Perkins. In her book, all of that was more than enough reason to place him in an interrogation room and get him to talk.

CHAPTER TWENTY FIVE

Once again, Ava could feel the stare of everyone in the Seventeenth Precinct as she and Pawlowski brought Isaac O'Hare into the building. She did her best to ignore it, lowering her head and directing O'Hare to the back, where the interrogation rooms were located.

"Just keep walking," Ava said, honestly not sure if she was speaking to Pawlowski or O'Hare.

She feared that O'Hare would start cackling again, as he'd done during the cab ride over, drawing more unnecessary attention to them. He managed to remain stable, though, and they made it to the hallway at the other side of the room without incident.

However, when Pawlowski opened the door to the interrogation room, a voice called out to them. It was a familiar male voice, the sound of Captain Miller sounded quite aggravated.

"Detective Gold? A word?"

Ava turned to face him and could tell by the stern look on his face that arguing or pleading her case would not be helpful. Instead, she turned back to Pawlowski and gave her a little nod. She watched as her new partner led O'Hare into the interrogation room. She did so quickly, as if fearing Miller would call her name as well.

Ava headed over to Miller, who was standing by the intersection of the hallway and the larger floor where the bullpen resided. She was slightly relieved when he didn't instantly lead her back towards his office. Her hope was that he wouldn't act irrationally or try to start an argument while they were standing in front of the entire precinct.

"Yes, sir?"

"Who's this?" he asked, nodding to the now-closed interrogation room door.

"Isaac O'Hare. He's one of the names we found on Perkins's list of clients in his office. We spoke with the coroner and discovered a strange bit of fabric that had been taken off the body, gripped in his hand. O'Hare owned—or, rather *once* owned—a textile mill that made the exact same kind of fabric. When we spoke to him, he came right out and told us he'd lost everything because of O'Hare and the crash."

"And that was enough to cuff him and bring him in?" Miller asked, incredulous.

"No, sir. We arrested him because he drew a gun on me."

"Oh. I see." He seemed confused and first, and then concerned. "Was anyone hurt?"

"No, sir. We're fine."

"Good. Detective Gold, I fear that if nothing comes out of this interrogation, we're going to have to remove you and Pawlowski from the case. There's just not enough justification for keeping it open while everything points to suicide."

"I understand, sir."

He stood still for a moment, watching her closely as if he was sure she was going to argue. When she said nothing, he gave a curt nod and then turned away, heading back for his office. She'd known this would happen but felt disappointed all the same. They hadn't even been given until the end of the day—which was only two hours away, but it still stung.

She entered the interrogation room, walking in just as Pawlowski was finishing up with a question.

"...two nights ago? Were you anywhere near the Chrysler Building?"

"What in God's holy name would I be visiting that place for? An ugly eyesore on the city if you ask me. So...no. No, I was nowhere near the Chrysler Building two nights ago. In fact, I was nowhere near that side of town."

"Can you tell us where you were?" Pawlowski asked. Ava remained quiet, letting Pawlowski run with it.

O'Hare thought about his answer for a while and then shrugged. "Guess it makes no difference now, if I'm already under arrest. If you must know, I was with an old friend of mine down in Harlem, having some drinks."

"A speakeasy?" Pawlowski asked.

"No. At his place. He'd gotten it off of someone else. It was some awful rotgut, that's for sure, but it did the trick."

"How long were you there?"

"I don't...Jesus, I don't recall. The last few days have been a blur. Hell, the last few weeks. I mean...it's all been such a whirlwind, there are days I forget to even change my damned clothes!"

"Well, try to remember," Ava said.

She could see him thinking hard. Finally, he said, "I think I was there pretty much all day and night. My wife…she's been insufferable since we had to close the mill and shop down. I've been staying with my friend for a while here and there."

"We'll need his name."

"No, I don't think so. No way I'm going to let you go over there under the guise of clearing my story only to bust him for having alcohol."

"And what about the gun?"

"What about it?"

"Why did you have a gun on you when we came by?" Pawlowski asked. "It almost seems like you were waiting for someone in particular."

He let out the same chuckle he'd voiced several times since they'd come into contact with him. "No. Just keeping it on hand in case I ever get the courage to end my life."

Ava watched as Pawlowski considered this answer. She took several moments before she spoke again and when she did, Ava wasn't sure exactly where she was headed with the interrogation.

"You said you've been staying at your friend's house here and there, correct?"

"That's right."

"What about clothes? Do you have a change of clothes on you?"

He laughed once more. It was really starting to get on Ava's nerves and started to support the idea that maybe this *was* their man. He certainly wasn't in his right mind, and he didn't seem to be taking any of this seriously.

"You crazy broad. I just told you I have half a mind to kill myself. You think I give a damn about my clothes? I've been wearing these same clothes for nearly a week now."

Standing behind her partner, Ava could see Pawlowski sigh. She nodded and turned to Ava with a strange look on her face. "Can I speak to you outside, Detective Gold?"

Ava nodded, and both women left the room to step out into the hallway. Pawlowski closed the door behind them and stepped to the right, not too far away from where Ava and Miller had spoken just moments before.

"You heard him," Pawlowski said. "He hasn't changed his clothes in several days."

"Yeah?"

"Well, did you see his shoes?"

"No, I didn't really pay attention to them."

"I know it's a long shot," Pawlowski said, "but they look like they could be a match for that print we saw out on that beam at the Chrysler Building."

Ava knew it was indeed a long shot, especially because a photographer had never been sent up to document the site. And even if she and Pawlowski could confirm that the shoe matched the print, it wouldn't be enough.

"That *is* a long shot." As she said this, another thought occurred to Ava. She'd felt the edges of the theory while speaking with O'Hare in the interrogation room, but it only now presented itself as a full-formed thought. "Hear me out, for a second...."

"What? You don't think it's him? The shoes...I know it's flimsy at best, but..."

She shrugged, cutting her own self off. Ava wondered if her partner had come to the same conclusions she had just seconds ago.

"O'Hare is suicidal. He admitted to thinking of killing himself twice already. Why would a man murder someone by shoving them off a building and then approach the brink of killing himself two days later?"

"Maybe killing someone pushed him even further," Pawlowski suggested. "Maybe losing everything was the crack in the foundation and then taking another person's life split it."

"That's a good theory," Ava said, thinking it over. But even then, something still didn't feel right. "But why the Chrysler Building? O'Hare has no connection to it, even if Perkins did, in a small way."

"When you put the Chrysler Building into it, it all does sort of fall apart, huh?" Pawlowski asked. "So...what do we do now? We're almost out of time."

"Maybe. Even if O'Hare isn't our killer, he *did* pull a gun on a cop. We can hold him on that for a while...paint it as if we're still questioning him about Perkins while he's here. That might buy us some more time."

"Time for what?"

"To figure out *why* the Chrysler Building. Through this whole thing, it's been the big, glaring tower at the center of all of this."

Pawlowski gave her a strange look, punctuated with a frown. "Jesus, Gold...you're talking about the building as if *it's* a suspect."

A smile touched Ava's lips, but only briefly.

Ava's eyes widened a bit as she pointed her index finger at Pawlowski. "You might just be on to something there."

"What?" Pawlowski asked as Ava was already starting to move to the bullpen and the front doors beyond. "What are you talking about?"

"The Race to the Sky," Ava said. "I think we'll find our answer in that."

And though Pawlowski clearly wasn't quite tracking with her, she followed Ava all the same—back out through the doors and hurrying down the streets in search of answers once again.

CHAPTER TWENTY SIX

By the time they'd managed to catch a cab, Ava still had no clear idea of where they needed to go. She felt they needed to learn more about the so-called Race to the Sky, to get a better understanding of the sort of people that were involved in it. The title itself was almost misleading—it sounded like a fun and friendly competition of sorts among men with far too much ego and money. That's why her first instinct was to head right back to 40 Wall Street, to see if they could have another conversation with Mr. White.

This was the address she gave the cab driver and they were headed that way when she started processing everything out loud. She was starting to understand that she and Pawlowski were a bit more similar than either of them wanted to admit and she hoped Pawlowski could add a degree of balance to her ideas.

"The Race to the Sky," she said. "Sounds almost like a cute little game, right?"

"I suppose," Pawlowski said.

"I think it might be a little misleading. Just sounds like men measuring their…well, their egos, among other things. But we already know that it was competitive enough to have people from the Chrysler Building trying to get people at 40 Wall Street to divert finds and investments their way. And if that's the case, it means there was a lot of money tied up in it—during a time when there isn't much money to go around."

"So you think the killer is wrapped up in the Race to the Sky somehow?"

"I think it's worth digging into," Ava said. What she thought but did not say was: *And I think it's a thread we should have pulled a little harder at from the get-go.* "White told me that the spire was put on top of the Chrysler Building without any sort of announcements or news beforehand. It was done almost in secret. And that spire made it officially the tallest building in the world. Secrecy like that…yeah, I think it's pretty competitive."

"And the Empire State Building is the other building involved," Pawlowski said. "We haven't heard anything about that location yet."

"Maybe that's where we need to look, then. Maybe there's some link between Perkins and the Empire State Building we simply haven't seen."

"And you know," Pawlowski said. "There's something else that occurred to me back at the station when we were talking about O'Hare being suicidal. It made me think about Mrs. Perkins. I don't remember her specific words, but she mentioned how one of Alfred's worries was that in this crash, there would be very little left to make sure he could take care of her. Or something like that, right?"

"Yes, I recall that."

"Well I don't know the laws or the regulations, but I'd assume that a man that takes his own life isn't going to reap the rewards of whatever life insurance he has lined up, right?"

"That's a good point," Ava said. "And I think it also points to his refusal to work with the folks at the Chrysler Building in terms of sending clients their way. He didn't want any sort of drama or obstacles. He was wanting to take care of himself and his wife."

"Not the sound of a suicidal man at all if you ask me," Pawlowski pointed out.

There was a renewed sense of urgency to each of them when the cab stopped in front of the building at 40 Wall Street. When they stepped inside, Ava looked at her watch and saw that it was 4:19. She hoped having O'Hare back at the precinct would buy them some time but as far as she was concerned, she was still counting on five o' clock being the end of their time limit to prove Alfred Perkins had not died by his own hand.

They walked into the front door and approached the counter, which was now a very familiar scene to Ava. This would be, after all, the third time she'd come here in the past two days. She stopped by the counter out of impulse and barely even looked at the woman sitting there when she flashed her badge and said, "NYPD. We need to speak with Mr. White."

"Oh, hold on a second," the sheepish woman behind the counter said. "I'm sorry, but Mr. White is gone for the day."

Ava halted at the end of the counter and turned around quickly. "Do you know where he's gone?"

"I don't. Something to do with a family appointment. If you'd like to set up a time to speak with him tomorrow, I'd be happy to take a message."

"This is time sensitive," Ava said. "I think we'd be okay without him, actually. I simply need to have another look in Alfred Perkins's office."

"Oh, I see," the receptionist said. "Well, you're welcome to, but you should know that most of his things have been cleared out. His wife and some movers took care of most of it today."

Ava was discouraged at first but then figured they could just pay a visit to Mrs. Perkins. For all they knew, she may know a bit about any involvement her husband might have had with other individuals taking part in the Race to the Sky.

"Thank you," Ava said, already turning back for the doors.

"I'm not sure what you're looking for, but there were a few things left behind at the request of Mr. White," the receptionist said. "Things concerning current projects still in process, and contacts of certain clients. If you're looking for recent business-related items, it's likely still here."

"Is it still in his office?"

"Yes," the receptionist said. She then reached down below the counter and opened up a drawer. Seconds later, she retrieved a key and handed it to Ava.

Both Ava and Pawlowski gave their thanks and head directly for the stairs. As they climbed then, Pawlowski said, "What do you know? We actually caught a break."

"Not only that," Ava said, "but the bulk of the digging has already been done. Anything recent and related to current projects means that anything related to the Chrysler Building or the Empire State Building is going to be in the things that were left behind."

They made their way to the fourth-floor hallway, making a direct course for Perkins's office. The door had been left open, but everything except the desk and a single bookshelf had been removed. The only exception was a small box sitting on the desk. When Ava looked inside, she found a series of papers that looked to have all been clipped together. Among the papers were a few notebooks and a smaller, leather book.

Ava's attention went to the leather book right away, merely because it looked more important and official than anything else. A childish impulse at its core, it proved to pay off almost right away. When she opened it up, she found that it was Alfred Perkins's planner. When she opened it to the first page, she saw that it started a little over eight months ago, at the start of the year.

"His planner," she said, scanning through the pages and coming to a stop when she reached the days from several weeks ago.

Many of the notes were very brief and written in a way that seemed almost like code but was likely just Perkins's own shorthand way of saving time and space on the pages. *Mtg w Deringer, 2. Bank apt w Herber Bros, 11.* She did see two entries from six weeks ago that read: *Mtg w Albrecht, 3:30 – CB.*

Albrecht, Ava thought. *Albrecht, CB. That clearly stands for Chrysler Building, given Albrecht's association with it.* As she scanned through them, a few dates from three weeks ago caught her eye. There were two entries within the same week and then another listing one week prior to his death.

The listings read: *Lunch – Fairfax – ESB.* The third listing was exactly the same, only it ended with an underlined question mark.

"ESB," Ava said. "That could be an abbreviation for Empire State Building, right?"

Pawlowski was thumbing through one of the notebooks that had been left behind. She nodded her agreement, but it was clear that her attention was on whatever she was looking at.

"Could be," she said. "But hey, I think this is something sort of like a contacts list. They're sort of scrawled all over the place. Some of them have little notes that seem to be when he first met them—or when he last met them. I'm not sure."

"That's excellent" Ava said. "See if you can find the name Fairfax. I've got an entry in his schedule—several of them actually—where he was supposed to meet someone by the name of Fairfax. And they're denoted with *ESB.*"

Pawlowski did as she was asked and within just a few seconds, she nodded and placed the notebook on the desk. "Right there," she said. "Henry Fairfax. And beside his name is one interesting word."

Ava looked at the listing and saw what Pawlowski was talking about. Written by Fairfax's name was the word *Empire.*

"And there's the connection to the Empire State Building," Ava said.

Pawlowski picked up the notebook with the phone numbers and started for the door. "The way I see it, we have a name and a phone number. I say we call and meet with him now."

Ava agreed one hundred percent, reminding herself that they had a man in an interrogation room that, while he had indeed pointed a gun at her, was not at all guilty of the murder they were investigating.

They made their way back downstairs, back to the receptionist. For the second time in the past two days, Ava asked to borrow the phone. The woman behind the desk handed it over eagerly, her wide and excited eyes indicating that she could sense the urgency behind the call Ava was about to make.

While Pawlowski thanked the woman, Ava found the number listed for Fairfax and placed the call. It was answered on the third ring by a woman that had a rather rough, haggard voice.

"Mr. Fairfax's office."

"This is Detective Ava Gold with the NYPD," she said. "I need to speak with Mr. Fairfax, please."

"He's not in the office right now. Might I ask what this is about?"

Ava figured there was no sense in tipping a potential suspect off as to why the police might want to speak to him, so she decided to make a cover story on the fly. Not only a story to cover her backside, but to perhaps entice Fairfax to speak with them and to have his secretary make sure she did her best to connect them.

"I've been tasked with looking into a recent suicide at an investment firm," she said. "It seems that when this man took his own life, he owed many people some money—something to do with construction contracts and investments. The details are quite murky. But we do have a list of people that he owed money to. His employers are adamant that we make sure every penny is paid, but needed the police to sort of look over it to make sure everything was done by the book. And it just so happens that Mr. Fairfax's name is on that list."

"Oh my," the woman on the other end said. "Well, I'm certainly sorry to hear about the suicide, that's for sure. But I also know that Mr. Fairfax will want to know this as soon as possible. I'll be sure to have him call you at the very first chance he gets."

"Well, the day is coming to a close," Ava said. "Do you know where he might be? Maybe I can speak with him face to face."

"Oh, sure. He's been over at the Empire State Building all afternoon. He had some business over there and, just between you, me, and the wire, I think he just likes to be around the construction."

"That's an enormous help. Thank you so much."

Ava hung up the phone so quickly that she barely had time to hear the secretary as she said: "You're welcome."

Ava looked to Pawlowski with a nervous smile and said, "Looks like we're headed to the Empire State Building after all."

CHAPTER TWENTY SEVEN

Ava had driven by the Empire State Building multiple times, but just like with the Chrysler Building, she'd never had any reason to step inside. She knew through the news that it, like the Chrysler Building, was not yet completed. From what she understood, there were some businesses being conducted out of its lower floors and offices, but it was not yet the large, thriving epicenter of business it was expected to be when it was finally complete.

When the cab dropped them off, Ava studied the exterior. From what she could tell, most of the construction was much higher up on the left side. She craned her neck to look at the uncompleted floors far, far above her head as she and Pawlowski made their way inside.

If Ava had never seen the active construction outside, she would have never known the place was incomplete. The lobby waiting for them beyond the main doors was pristine, although a bit empty. Ava attributed this to the fact that it was the end of the business day, her watch now reading 4:51.

There were two people moving around behind the front desk that sat just in front of the main doors after an expansive lobby opened the place up. One was a man, the other a woman, and they both greeted Ava and Pawlowski warmly.

"How can I help you?" the man asked. He was a bit older but still made very little attempt to hide the fact that he was admiring Pawlowski's form.

"We just spoke with the secretary over at Henry Fairfax's office," Ava said. "We were told Mr. Fairfax was here."

"That he is," the man said, delighted to be of service. "If you'll just walk around the lobby to the right, you'll see a short hallway that leads back to a few elevators. Take those up to the sixth floor and you'll see a conference room along the main hallway. You'll find him there. Now, there's a chance he's still in a meeting, but I don't think so. I think just about everyone in that meeting has left for the day."

"Thanks so much," Pawlowski said, smiling at the man. She'd apparently noticed his lingering gaze and was trying to use it to her advantage. Ava wondered if that was why the man and woman had not bothered asking who they were or why they needed to speak with Fairfax.

They followed the directions and came to the elevator easily enough. As it rose up to the sixth floor, it was far too similar to the ride up in the Chrysler Building—only much shorter. Ava was relieved when it came to a stop and the doors slid open in front of them.

The space within the hallway was wide and open, nearly making Ava forget about the sprawling amount of floors ascending over her head. When they came to the conference room, they found the door standing open, revealing one of the biggest rooms Ava had ever seen. The two tables pushed together in the center were littered with notebooks, binders, and papers—some of which looked like blueprints. Despite the mess, there were only three people in the room.

Ava raised her hand to knock but found herself frozen for a moment. As she looked in at the three men, she found herself focused immediately on one of them more than the others. They all appeared to be middle-aged—somewhere between forty-five and fifty.

The one standing closest to them had Ava's full attention. And as she stood there, momentarily frozen, Pawlowski's voice spoke softly behind her.

"Gold…you see it, right?"

Ava only nodded as she knocked. By the time she'd been able to knock, all three of the men had turned her way. Two of them were smiling. But the man that she'd taken instant notice of did not.

This man wore a nice, navy-colored suit. The jacket was open in a casual manner and his tie was loosened, a sign of the day coming to an end. But what had caught Ava's attention was the button-down shirt he wore beneath it. It was an off-white with a subtle cross-stitched pattern of diamonds.

It was the exact same material and design of the fabric that had been found clutched in Alfred Perkins's hand. At first, it seemed like one of those too-good-to-be-true moments. Surely, she was seeing things, *making* herself see a link that wasn't there.

But then something O'Hare had said rocketed through her head.

"…it's all been such a whirlwind, there are days I forget to even change my damned clothes!"

Maybe, if this was indeed Fairfax, he'd been living that same sort of life as of late, trying to salvage his own fortunes as well as those of his clients and ignoring the simpler luxuries in life.

"Hello, ladies," one of the other men said. He was stacking up a few papers, giving them a curious glance. "Anything we can do for you?"

"Yes, actually," Ava said. "We need to speak with Mr. Fairfax."

When it was clear no one was going to leave the room, Pawlowski spoke up and said, "Privately."

The man stacking papers chuckled at this, giving Fairfax a devilish grin. The third man laughed a bit, too, but was more agreeable. He nodded to Ava and Pawlowski without even asking who they were and made his exit. When he did, he turned to Fairfax and the other man, giving them a wave.

And in doing so, he confirmed it: the man with the torn garment was indeed Fairfax.

"No, really," Pawlowski said. "In private."

"Can I ask what for?" Fairfax asked, finally speaking for the first time.

"No, no, just give me a moment," the other man said. He gathered up his papers and placed them in a briefcase that also sat on the desk. As he did this, Fairfax studied Ava and Pawlowski, still saying nothing. Ava could see the concern in his face and waited for him to request that his friend stay behind. But he remained quiet as the man said his goodbyes and made his way out. Ava and Pawlowski parted through the doorway as he left.

"Okay," Fairfax said. "Enough of this guessing. Who are you, and what do you need?"

Ava showed her badge first, then Pawlowski. "We need to speak to you about any dealings you had with a man by the name of Alfred Perkins."

"Perkins? Yes…I know him. He works over on 40 Wall Street."

"Have you ever worked alongside him?" Ava asked.

"Not officially, no."

"And when was the last time you saw him?" Pawlowski asked.

"I don't know. Maybe a week or so? We had lunch."

"Have you ever met with him over at the Chrysler Building?" Ava asked.

His facial response pretty much gave him away. He looked shocked and terrified, as if someone had slapped him hard across the face. "No," he said. "No, I don't believe so."

"Have *you* ever been to the Chrysler Building?"

Fairfax looked very confused, but Ava was pretty sure it was an act. He slowly started to pace along the opposite side of the desk. When he reached their side, he took a seat and looked up at them. "I'm sorry…what *is* this all about?"

"That's a nice shirt," Ava said. "Under the jacket, I mean. Did you tear it recently?"

This time, his eyes went wide and there was no hiding the fact that he was not only scared, but deeply confused. "What?"

Ava reached into her pocket but didn't pull out the scrap of fabric yet. "Mr. Fairfax, were you aware that Alfred Perkins died two nights ago?"

Fairfax didn't answer. In fact, he was starting to look a little angry. He kept looking back and forth between Ava and Pawlowski. To Ava, it almost looked like he was sizing them up. From where he sat, he had a fairly direct line to the door. Pawlowski could easily step in his way if it came to that and from there, it would be a simple two-on-one confrontation.

"Everything about the death suggests it was a suicide—that Perkins jumped from the very top of the Chrysler Building. But there were just enough uncertainties to make us look a bit closer. And in our digging, we discovered that *this* was found in his hand when he fell."

She removed the scrap from her pocket and tossed it on the table.

"We also know that he was meeting with you to discuss something related to the Empire State Building. You may be interested to know that he was also meeting with people from the Chrysler Building."

"So, you're accusing me of *what*, exactly?"

"I'm not quite sure yet," she said. "But I sure would like to take a closer look at that shirt of yours."

"Let's see it, Fairfax," Pawlowski said. "Take the jacket off and untuck your shirt."

"Absolutely not."

"Do it," Ava said, "or we're going to arrest you and walk you out in front of those men that just walked out of here. You'll be in handcuffs, caught by two dames. Not a good look for you, for sure."

"Fine," he hissed. He stood up from the chair and eyed them both with such malice that Ava could feel it burning into her. He started to remove his jacket, taking his right arm out first and then working on his left.

It was then, as he still had one arm in the jacket, that he moved so unexpectedly and in a strange way, that it caught both Ava and

Pawlowski off guard. He stripped the jacket off of his left arm and, in the same motion, threw it as hard as he could at Ava. It felt silly but was also so out of the blue that it took Ava a full two seconds to understand what had happened. She slapped the jacket away as she felt Fairfax rushing by her.

She got it away from her face just in time to see Fairfax collide with Pawlowski at the door. He slammed Pawlowski against the wall but even then, Pawlowski managed to drive her elbow into the side of his head. It sent Fairfax stumbling to the side, but he managed to deliver a quick left-handed jab as he staggered and caught his balance against the doorframe. The punch connected, catching Pawlowski in the top of the head. As she hit the wall again and tried to keep from sliding to the floor, Fairfax took off into the hallway.

"You okay?" Ava asked as she rushed to Pawlowski.

"Yeah. I should have got him. I'm…"

"But you're okay?"

"Yeah…"

Ava could tell that Pawlowski was more embarrassed than anything else, so the decision to leave her and pursue Fairfax was an easy one. She made her way back down the hall and saw Fairfax disappearing through a door marked STAIRS. A smart move, she thought, to not wait for the elevator.

"Freeze, Fairfax!" she bellowed.

But Fairfax had no intention of freezing at all. He rocketed through the doorway and she could hear his heavy footfalls tearing up the stairs.

Up? Ava thought. *Really? Why are you going up?*

She drew her sidearm as she came to the stairwell door, opening it up and quickly pivoting inside. Fairfax was not there waiting for her. Instead, she could hear his feet above her, stomping further up the stairs. She gave chase, rushing up the stairs and taking them two at a time. Her primary hope was that she was simply in much better shape than Fairfax and she'd be able to catch up to him. She supposed his goal was to go up several floors and perhaps lose her in the maze of construction. And once there, maybe he'd try to bait her into a situation where he could pitch her off the side—much like he seemed to have done to Alfred Perkins.

With this possibility in the back of her mind, she continued treading upwards. She ran as fast as she could, realizing just how close Fairfax's footfalls were starting to sound against the concrete steps. She'd lost count of how may flights she'd climbed. Nine? Ten? She just didn't know. It may have been as many as a dozen.

What she did know was that she could now hear Fairfax's breathing, coming hard and labored. If she could hear that even over the thunderous booming of their footfalls, he must be just a flight or two ahead.

Apparently, he knew this as well. The sound of his rampaging feet came to a stop, interrupted by the sound of a pause, a door opening, and then more footsteps, only fainter this time.

She arrived at the next landing just in time to see the door leading back into the building closing. The small sign by the edge of the doorframe read: 21. She was astounded as she opened the door and entered the hallway. The chase had gone by quickly and her legs felt like they were pumping fire, but she had not expected to have climbed so high so fast.

The hallway wasn't completed. The foundations were up, as well as the many levels over her head, but the walls weren't finished. There were studs and foundational boards set in place for most of it, but there were also open, empty spaces here and there, allowing access to the exterior of the building for the workers. Through those breaks, she could see beams and struts, just like she'd seen near the top of the Chrysler Building.

At first, she didn't see him. There were several rooms to her right—or, rather, the shapes of rooms, just as unfinished as the walls to her left. If he was hiding in any of them, she'd spot him easily enough. And if it came down to a fight, she did have a gun. Not that she thought she'd need it.

But then, just as she started down the hallway, she saw him. He was about a quarter of the way down, standing on one of the exposed beams that was visible through the access point to the exterior. As he stood on it, the wind whipped at his hair and his shirt. Ironically, his shirt had come untucked in the chase; the wind caused his shirt to flap in a way that clearly showed the torn section along the back.

Ava stopped walking for a moment as their eyes locked. She then started moving so slowly that it was barely even progress at all. She needed to get closer to him—needed to make sure she got the arrest.

"Don't do it, Mr. Fairfax," she said. She had to raise her voice a bit to be heard over the wind.

"You'd rather I come with you and go to jail?"

Ava said nothing. She continued to inch her way forward. She also made a show of holstering her weapon and then placed her hands in the air. "Is that an admission?" she asked. "Do you need to go to jail?"

"I'd change it if I could. I was just…I was so mad. And the opportunity was right there. I had to do it. And when I did…Christ…he reached out and grabbed me. Tore the tail of my shirt and nearly pulled me right off the side of the building with him. Thank God this shirt is cheap." He laughed nervously at this, and the sound of it made Ava wonder if he'd really jump. He simply sounded far too scared to do it.

"Come back in here," Ava said. "Come back in and we can talk about it."

"I killed a man," he said. "There *is* no talking, right? It's jail."

"Yes. Very likely. But isn't that better than death? You'll still have family and friends. You'll still have *life*. The idea that she was trying to talk him out of jumping when she now knew for certain what he'd done was odd. It made her feel very uncertain of herself.

"I…I can't," he said. "I'm scared to move."

Of course, Ava thought. "Hold on," she said.

She moved forward making sure not to peer out through the opening to the beams. Sure, this was nothing compared to the heights she'd looked down from at the Chrysler Building, but she was still twenty-one stories in the air. The wind slipped in through the opening, catching her hair and blowing it about. She stepped to the opening and extended her hand to him. Even without looking down, she felt a bit dizzy.

Fairfax was weeping as he slowly reached for her hand. She did her best to keep eye contact with him and it was because of this that she saw the sudden change in his eyes.

"I'm so sorry," he said.

"Wh—" Ava started to say.

Then he jumped.

Ava acted reflexively, reaching out with both hands to grab him by the shoulder and upper arm. She took hold of him and leaned back instantly, trying to counteract the pull of gravity. For a moment, it worked. Fairfax stumbled back along the beam toward the opening back into the building. But then, in the last moment, his right foot missed the beam and found open air. He went pitching over to the side, and the sudden shift also pulled Ava.

She was falling, too. And as the open air yawned before her and the city streets waited twenty-one stories below, Ava knew she had to make a decision: let him go, or fall with him.

Gritting her teeth in frustration and feeling her heart about to burst with terror in her chest, Ava made her decision.

CHAPTER TWENTY EIGHT

In the sickening moment Ava decided to let Fairfax fall, she felt an incredible pressure latch on to her shoulders. The shock of it loosened her grip on Fairfax but when she realized it was a set of steady, stabilizing hands at her shoulders, she gripped him even harder.

Ava was pulled back hard and fast—so hard that when she was back in the hallway and her feet were on solid ground, she collided with one of the temporary walls behind her. Her shoulder and left foot slammed into the wall, knocking holes in it. Plaster and dust puffed out almost comically.

Fairfax was at her feet, having collapsed to the ground in a sobbing mess. Standing just behind him and taking a very cautious step away from the exterior access point within the wall, Pawlowski looked like she was about to be sick.

"Thank you," Ava gasped. The totality of what had almost happened hadn't caught up to her yet. She'd almost died and, even if she'd managed to make it out, would have been responsible for Fairfax falling. But Pawlowski had prevented all of that from happening.

They both looked down at the floor at the sobbing mess that was Henry Fairfax. Ava realized she had no cuffs, but watched as Pawlowski got hers out.

"I got a confession," Ava said. "He's under arrest."

As Pawlowski did her best to cuff him, Ava attempted to help but realized that her entire body was trembling from what she'd just experienced. She did what she could to help while also noticing that the blow Fairfax had dealt out to Pawlowski on his way out of the conference room.

"You okay?" Pawlowski asked, looking at Ava.

"Yeah, I just need a second."

"Apparently, he does, too," she said, nodding to a still-sitting Fairfax. Ava wasn't even sure he knew the cuffs were on him.

As she gathered her wits and nerves again, Ava started to consider what may have led Fairfax to do what he'd done to Alfred Perkins. She supposed he could have been looking for people that might have some stake in the Race to the Sky to sabotage the construction of the Chrysler Building. After all, Perkins's death had come *very* soon after that spire had been placed on top of the building. Maybe there had been an argument between them and it had resulted in Fairfax pushing Perkins off. It made some sense, though not a lot, but it was all she could think of in that moment.

After a minute or so, she trusted her legs to walk again. Fairfax had come around a bit, too, but was looking back and forth between Ava and Pawlowski as if he had just woken up from a particularly bad dream.

"Come on," Ava said, grabbing him beneath his left armpit. "Up we go."

"I'm sorry…so…sorry," he said. "For you, for Perkins…for…"

Pawlowski took him beneath the other armpit and he managed to find his feet. He didn't fight them as they led him back to the stairwell. And even though he was still dazed and half-crying in itching breaths, he was actually of some help by the time they'd reached the stairwell landing on the seventeenth floor.

"The elevator…on this floor…"

He was even speaking like a man that was half asleep. As they stepped out into the finished, completed hallways along the seventeenth floor, Fairfax's footsteps became more like shuffles. He still moved of his own accord, but it took more prodding and urging. Ava wondered if he might be slipping into some sort of shock over what he'd nearly done four floors over their heads.

Ava glanced over to Pawlowski as they led Fairfax to the elevators. The floor was empty and very quiet, giving off an overall eerie feeling. Pawlowski returned her glance and offered a tired smile. The bruise on her forehead was growing purple and starting to swell into a knot. Still, there was a look of pride and satisfaction in Pawlowski's eyes.

Neither of them said anything as they came to the elevator. Ava called it up and when they stepped on, guiding Fairfax along with them, Ava realized how oddly comfortable the silence between them felt.

***

As Ava looked at Fairfax sitting at the table in the interrogation room, she was well aware of Miller's presence in the room. Captain Miller was standing in the corner and had not said a single word since he'd entered. Ava wondered if he was tired from all the interrogation

145

room juggling, having officially sent Isaac O'Hare home just twenty minutes ago when Fairfax had been brought in.

Meanwhile, Pawlowski sat down in the chair on Ava's side of the table, holding a bag of ice to her forehead.

"You told me something while you were standing out on that beam," Ava said, her eyes set on Fairfax. "You admitted to something. I need you to repeat that."

Fairfax was surprisingly at ease. He'd been agreeable and mostly obedient ever since he'd stopped crying up on the twenty-first floor. There were still signs of that slight daze in his eyes and the way he moved.

He did repeat it, but he also went into more detail. And, in doing so, he proved Ava's theory to be partially correct—but mostly wrong.

"We all got caught up in it…in that Race to the Sky, you know? We had supervisors and directors sniping investors from other property managers and construction crews. It was all over the place, trying to convince people where their money would be best spent and which building would prove to be the most successful—would bring the most business to the city. I was asked to…"

He stopped here and Ava watched him struggle with another bout of tears. He managed to hold them back for the most part, but his voice grew thinner as he kept going.

"I was asked to figure out a way to sabotage the final stages of the Chrysler Building. Nothing bad, just a setback that would reach the public's ears. And when they put that damn spire on, that seemed like a great opportunity. I knew some of the construction guys, so I knew a way to the stairs that would take me behind the security desk inside the building, you know? I had asked Perkins to meet me up there, that I had a job opportunity to for him. I asked if he could get someone to sort of…I don't know…*infiltrate* the construction crew…maybe knock that spire loose."

"And did he agree to it?" Miller asked, speaking up for the first time.

"No. In fact, he seemed insulted that I suggested it. We got into a screaming match at each other and it occurred to me…it occurred to me that the Chrysler Building was such a big deal because it was the single building in the entire Race to the Sky that could boast that not a single person had died while it was being built. And as we were fighting up there, so high up in the sky, I just…I lost it. I stepped outside of my damned mind and…"

"You pushed him," Ava said.

The bluntness of the comment seemed to rock him and in that moment, she saw any stubborn façade fade from his expression. It made her think that anything they got out of him from this point on would be the truth. And when it came, it came quickly and as if he was almost *glad* to speak it.

"Well, we started throwing fists first. Things got carried away and I hit him with a board. He stumbled out and fell, but he caught a beam. I tried my best—even went out to see if I could help him, you know. I even went out on the beam he was clinging to but…it was too late. He fell. He fell, and I watched it happen. After that, I ran. I just…I didn't know what to do."

The room fell into silence after that. Miller was the one that broke it, asking a question that Ava hadn't even thought of yet. "Would you be willing to give us the names of the people that had you looking into this sabotage job?"

"I don't know. Maybe. Just…can I get some time alone, please?"

"We can manage that, I think," Miller said.

Ava gave Fairfax one last glance. She almost felt sorry for him. The pressure of this so-called Race to the Sky had clearly unhinged this man.

Miller opened the door and allowed Ava and Pawlowski to head out first. He waved them on to follow him to his office without saying a word. It was 6:30 in the afternoon now and there weren't as many people present to stare this time.

Miller didn't sit down behind his desk. Instead, he chose to sit along the edge of it with his arms crossed against his chest.

"Well, it wasn't the prettiest case I've ever seen but I admire you ladies sticking to your guns."

"Nah, that was mostly Gold," Pawlowski said. "I was ready to stop and call it a suicide yesterday afternoon."

Miller looked directly at Ava and smiled thinly. "I was pretty close to calling Minard and telling him I wanted out of this little experiment. But I'm glad I didn't. I'd heard about how hard-working you are and this just proved it. You proved a suicide was a murder *and* managed to uncover some shady dealings with this bullshit Race to the Sky." He nodded, let out a laugh, and then shrugged at them both.

"What is it, sir?" Pawlowski asked.

"Not bad for a first case together," he said. "I think the two of you may just have to get used to one another for a while. But for now…you're both welcome to go home. Gold, I know you've got a bit of a ride."

"Actually, sir, I think I'd like to stick around. Just, not for Fairfax."

"What for, then?"

She thought of the possibility of being partnered with Pawlowski and, in tandem, of possibly needing to move on from Frank and the life she'd started to build with him. The future was ahead of her, all questions, and possibilities. But before she could accept any of it, there was a part of her past she needed to wrap up.

"Could I have some time in your records department? There's something I'd like to look into."

"About this case?"

"No, sir. It's more of a personal matter."

Miller gave another shrug and said, "Help yourself."

She nodded her thanks and then looked to Pawlowski. Smiling, she said, "See you tomorrow?"

"If you're lucky," Pawlowski replied.

With that, Ava left Miller's office and went off in search of the records room within the Seventeenth Precinct. Even before she found it, she drew a name to the center of her mind—a peculiar name that had come from the mouth of a goon that had tried getting the best of her at a place where Jim Spurlock had been running an illegal casino.

Ms. Zebra. She recalled thinking in the moment she'd heard it that it would be an easy name to remember. She had that name, and she had a place called the Ash Lodge, a place that had matchbooks with its name on the front.

It was a good starting point. It was the most information she'd had since pursuing her husbands' killer and now, with a wide open future ahead of her, she felt more certain than ever that it was time to bring that painful part of her life to a close.

CHAPTER TWENTY NINE

Ava wasn't familiar enough with the people in the Seventeenth Precinct to just take records out. That's why she had a sheet of paper folded into her jacket pocket as she rounded the corner of a quiet and dark Manhattan Street at 11:05 that night.

She'd found quite a bit of information at the precinct and had then gone home to combine it with the notes she'd taken from her previous research. She hadn't made it home in time to tuck Jeffrey into bed, but she'd kissed him on his forehead before she left her apartment, leaving him in the good and safe hands of her father.

There had still been no sign of Frank.

She supposed it was just as well, considering what she was about to do.

Thanks to the night's research at the Seventeenth Precinct, she had learned a small amount on a woman that went by the moniker of Ms. Zebra. She'd also found two mentions of a place that suspects had referred to as the Ash Lodge. previous records she'd collected at her old precinct had given her one additional mention. From what she could tell, it was a bar that didn't exist, a speakeasy hiding in the secrets and shadows of New York nights.

She was taking a chance, assuming that if a man like Spurlock had a casino that he moved from place to place, then maybe he had a mobile speakeasy as well. The piece to figuring out where it might be came in the mentions of Ms. Zebra in the department records. Her real name was Madeline Zimmerman and she'd been a suspect in serval illegal gambling and alcohol supply operations. There were rumors of prostitution as well, but she'd never been formally charged with anything.

It had taken some digging and guesswork, but Ava had narrowed down her search for the Ash Lodge between two places based on the records that had mentioned Ms. Zebra's activities. One was out closer to Harlem, in a district that had seen many businesses shut down and pretty much ignored and neglected by the public. The other was a small furniture shop on the western rim of Manhattan, a shop once owned by

Madeline Zimmerman and then sold to a man named Al Freemont—a known associate of none other than Jim Spurlock—a little over eight months ago.

Ava eyed the furniture store now, from the opposite side of the street. She'd seen at least two people go in, entering through a side door. And because she'd seen this, she also knew that there was a man standing by the door. She assumed this meant the place was invitation only and that she'd need a card or password to get in. Ava, of course, had neither. But what she did have was a .38 revolver and a vicious right-hand jab.

She's dressed the part, just in case. As far as she was concerned, she would not go home empty-handed tonight. She needed to close this chapter before stepping into her future and she was prepared to do it at any cost. The success of the Perkins case still had her feeling that anything was possible, which made it a bit easier to confidently cross the street in her skimpy, sleeveless evening dress. It wasn't a stunning piece, but it had been too short for Clarence to be comfortable with her wearing when he'd been alive. It wasn't exactly the same thing the flappers were wearing these days, but she figured it would blend right in with those setting out for a night of debauchery. She also carried a little purse, which held nothing but a few single dollars and her .38.

She hurried across the road toward the store, mainly because that's how she'd seen others approaching—probably to avoid being seen by any late-night pedestrians or wandering cops. She did not let the presence of the man at the door deter her. She needed to seem like she belonged there, that she was asked to be there.

The man at the door was rather large, the bulk of his mass hidden in the black coat he wore and the shadows of the slightly beveled doorway. He smiled at her in the darkness. "Hey there, darlin'. I just need the password."

She tried the first thing that came to her. If it didn't work, she had a backup plan.

"Ash Lodge."

The man's smile faltered right away, and he shook his head. "I don't know what you're trying to pull, but you—"

Ava delivered a quick and brutal jab to the man's throat. His words cut out but he barely staggered back. As a follow-up, she planted a firm kick to the man's knee and then brought her own knee up in recovery, slamming it into his crotch. This dropped the man like a rock. As he swayed on his knees, fumbling around near his belt for a gun Ava saw glistening in the faint streetlights, she delivered two more punches—another jab to his face and then a stunted uppercut that caused the man's chin and teeth to make a musical clicking noise.

The uppercut stung her wrist a bit, but it did the job. The bouncer toppled over, knocked out cold. He lay against the side of the doorway, meaning that Ava had to step over him as she opened the door. She entered and closed the door quickly behind her so no one inside would see the big, motionless shape at the doorway.

As she closed it, she took a moment to look around and found herself impressed with what she saw. She was standing in what looked to be a back room of sorts, with a large, open floor. Six tables were set up along the floor, and a long desk was pushed close to the back wall. The desk served as a bar, with several tall glass bottles sitting on top. There were kerosene lanterns positioned throughout, giving the place a soft and warm glow. Some were positioned on the tables, and one in the center of the bar. She took three seconds to take it all in, also making a quick count of the bodies. Not wanting to seem out of place, she casually walked in the direction of the bar. She kept her head low, but not low enough to attract suspicion.

She counted eight people in all—five men and three women. The men were dressed to the nines, wearing their best suits. The women were wearing outfits that Ava thought *might* be just a step above undergarments. They were beautiful pieces, but they left hardly anything to the imagination.

As she neared the bar, she spotted a ninth person. Another woman stood behind the bar, dressed in the tightest black dress Ava had ever seen. She smiled at Ava with full, red lips as she approached the bar. Ava smiled back, taking note that at least two of the five men in the place were looking at her. One of them, though, was far too preoccupied by the doll on his lap to take much notice.

As Ava approached the bar, she also took note of the thin, fluffy boa around the woman's neck. It was colored white and black, merging almost perfectly with the dress. The black and white pattern wasn't *exactly* stripes, but it did bring to mind a zebra. Ava almost mentioned this to the woman, hoping to get her to inadvertently spill information, but she figured there was no sense in creating a situation where she might give herself away.

"Always nice to see a new face," the woman that may or may not be Ms. Zebra said.

"You don't get them often?" Ava asked, trying to play it cool.

"Oh, we get them from time to time. Mostly dames like you." She smirked at Ava and said, "What'll you have?"

Ava eyed the bottles and shrugged. "It's been so long, I really don't know. You choose for me."

"Peach moonshine it is," she said. "Made special by Mr. Spurlock's cousin down in Maryland."

"Where *is* Mr. Spurlock?" Ava asked. "I was hoping to see him…to thank him for the invitation."

"Oh, he's here. He's just…well, he's busy. Upstairs, I believe. But if this is your first night. I'm sure he'll swing by to say hello." The woman grabbed a glass from under the desk and filled it with clear liquid from one of the larger bottles on the desk. As she poured, it occurred to Ava that she had no idea if she was supposed to pay or if the invitation to this place meant that everything was on the house.

The woman slid the glass over to her. Ava was a bit shocked to find just how badly she wanted the drink. It smelled like straight gasoline but she drank in happily anyway. The woman behind the bar—presumably Ms. Zebra—smiled at her. "Burns, huh?"

Ava grimaced as she swallowed it down. "Yeah," she gasped. "You could say that." And as it burned, she tried to recall the last time she'd had a drink. She'd snuck one here and there when she'd been singing (much to Clarence's dismay) but those occurrences had been few and far between.

"Another?"

Ava had to catch her breath, blinking back tears. Jesus, but it burned. Still, there was a delightful taste to it and a pleasant warm feeling flushed through her.

"Yes, please," she said. "Another."

As Ms. Zebra took the glass back and began to refill it, a man's voice spoke up. It came from Ava's right and further back, from an area hidden in the darkness.

"Let's not send our new guests home too dizzy now, Ms. Zebra."

Ava realized her mistake right away. When she turned to seek out this new voice, she was not keeping her face lowered. So when she saw the man and he, in turn, saw her, there was no hiding her identity.

The man currently walking out of the darkness was Jim Spurlock. And the recognition that gleamed in his eyes with malicious intent made it clear that he knew exactly who she was. He walked over to the bar, undaunted by her presence. Ava felt herself wanting to go for her gun right away. But the number of witnesses in the place made the decision rather difficult. If she shot a man in front of all of them, she'd lose her job and likely spend some time in jail, no matter who the victim was.

Spurlock joined her at the bar, making sure to keep a few feet of space between them. For just a split second, he glanced in Ms. Zebra's direction. "Take a break, would you, love?"

Ms. Zebra said nothing. She simply set the glass of moonshine down and walked away. As she made her way out onto the floor, her black and white feathered boa fluttered slightly behind her.

As soon as she was gone, Spurlock leaned over and smiled widely at her. "You got a gun in that purse?"

"I do."

"Put it on the desk."

"Or what? I found you. *Again*. And you know why."

"Yes, I know why. I also know that you beat two of my best men yesterday as if they were nothing more than schoolyard bullies. But I have many more people at my disposal. Men that won't think twice about hurting a worrisome bitch like yourself in as many ways as I tell them to." He grinned again and said, "You *are* a treat on the eyes. Maybe there could be some pleasure before all of the pain. It really all depends on what you do right now. So…put the purse on the bar. Are you really planning to shoot me in front of all of these people?"

She didn't answer. But she did slowly put the purse on the bar. As she slowly set it there, she became aware of the silence in the place. Without turning to look, she knew that every eye in the so-called Ash Lodge was on them.

"No," she finally answered. "I'd rather just see you in jail for the rest of your life."

"Well, that's not going to happen. Detective Gold, I fear you made a very big mistake coming in here tonight."

Ava was running out of patience, no longer interested in talking. While she may not shoot him in front of everyone in the Ash Lounge, her right hand was still throbbing from the punches she'd distributed to bouncer—as if reminding her of her boxing skills.

"You decide, then," Ava said. "Because you're getting embarrassed one way or the other, and I—"

Spurlock moved quickly…much faster than Ava would have given him credit for. He faked a slap with his left hand, which Ava blocked easily. But in blocking the slap, she missed the motion to her left as

Spurlock grabbed the bottle of moonshine and brought it sailing across in a hard arc.

The glass jar slammed into the side of her head, shattering. The rich, pungent smell of the strong alcohol filled her nose and eyes as she fell to the floor. There was an explosion of pain in her head as she toppled to the floor but she barely had time to even register it. Spurlock delivered a kick that caught her squarely in the ribs. She knew at once that she was fortunate he was wearing dressier shoes; if he'd been wearing boots, he would have broken her ribs.

The unpredictability of his attack had her at a loss, as well as not knowing if anyone else in the room would take part. She was dimly aware of the sound of chairs being pushed back and hurried footfalls crossing the floor as she tried getting to her hands and knees.

Spurlock dished out another kick, but this one was more playful than anything else. He then dropped down to a knee and slapped her in the face. A moment later, he slapped her on her backside.

He leaned down slightly and spoke softly to her. "I'm going to take you upstairs, Detective. We're going to have some fun, you and I, but I imagine some of it will hurt you. But let's be honest…killing your husband and then having you in a way you'll never have him again…well, that's just too good to pass up."

Ava wasn't expecting the roar of rage that came out of her as she pushed herself up. To stop her, Spurlock once again slapped her. It was harder this time, and that curtain of pain in her head increased. She could feel blood trickling down her head as Spurlock grabbed her by the hair and yanked her up. Her scalp felt as if it were burning, but she looked past it. Spurlock had put such a beating on her that he'd gotten cocky. The idiot was actually helping her to her feet. Granted, the room was spinning, and there was blood trickling down into her right eye, but she was at least being brought to her feet.

"The rest of you," he said, looking out to the room, "are welcome to stay and enjoy your night. And if anyone breathes a word of this outside of here, I'll send people to find you and end you. Are we understood?"

He punctuated this with a laugh. And it was that sound—that pleased and humored sound of delight that came out of his throat—that gave Ava the spark she needed.

She planted her feet and attacked the only way her current position would allow. She braced herself, knowing it would hurt, and then sprang into action, She stiffened her back and tossed her head back as fast and as hard as she could. Even before the back of her head slammed into Spurlock's face, Ava's head was screaming in pain. But the brittle *thunk* sound of Spurlock's face being crushed helped her push past it.

As a follow-up, she tightened up her left arm and drove her elbow back. She'd forgotten just how short Spurlock was, so instead of striking him in the chest, she caught him just below the neck. She heard him gag right away, his grip on her hair now released.

Still dizzy and bleeding, Ava wheeled around instantly. She saw Spurlock in two forms—his true self and as a blurred copy because of the dizziness. She decided to aim for the center and hit whatever she could. She doled out two rapid-fire jabs, the first of which caught him right in the nose. The second clipped the side of his head and spun him around. He fell into the bar and even then, Ava did not let up.

Still roaring, she took two large strides over to the bar. This time it was Ava that grabbed Spurlock by the hair. She lifted his head up and then slammed it hard into the desk. The makeshift bar rattled and shook, sending two glasses to the floor where they shattered. He rebounded fiercely, his right hand reaching for her purse. Ava, driven by an anger and hatred she'd never experienced before, drove a knee up into Spurlock's lower back. As he was sent forward again, she brought her right elbow down on the wrist that was still reaching for her purse.

She felt his wrist break beneath the blow. When Spurlock screamed out, Ava head footfalls behind her. She turned and saw one of the men rushing forward. But when he saw the state of her face, he stopped and grimaced. She didn't blame him. She could feel her head radiating pain, could feel and now even smell the blood coursing down her face, and the sting of alcohol among her injuries. Her ribs ached, too, but they were a minor pain when compared to the hell inside her head.

The man's interruption gave Spurlock just enough time. He grabbed her purse and drew out the .38 with his left hand. Ava knew it was a senseless thing to do, but she lowered herself into a tackle position and charged. She'd get shot, but maybe the movement would spare her head or anything vital.

She charged and when the shot came, she was sure she was dead.

Her body slammed into Spurlock and they both crashed to the floor in front of the bar. She lay there, on top of him for a moment, trying to figure out where she'd been shot. Her head was still a world of pain, but she couldn't feel anything else that—

A man's voice broke her train of thought. It was a familiar voice and for a moment, she was sure she *had* been shot and was hallucinating during her final living moments.

"No one move," this male voice said. "You move, you get shot."

Groaning, Ava rolled away from Spurlock. In doing so, she saw the large, gaping hole high on the right side of his stomach. He was gasping for breath and blinking rapidly at the ceiling.

Ava looked towards the voice and nearly started to weep.

Frank Wimbly stood just inside the door with his gun drawn. He was moving it slowly around the room, his eyes frantically moving back and forth between the patrons and Ava.

"Are you okay?" he asked her. "Christ, he did a number on you…"

"I'll be fine," she said. She slowly got to her feet, having to use the makeshift bar for support. Her legs were indeed a bit wobbly but she managed to take the gun from the floor where Spurlock had dropped it.

"How'd you…?" she started to ask.

"You got cuffs?" Frank asked. She wasn't sure, but it looked like he was on the verge of crying.

"Yeah," Ava said. Her voice sounded distant, far away. Maybe drowned out by the roaring waves of pain in her head. "I've got c…"

Her legs suddenly gave out. She was aware of Frank calling her name, but everything went black. She was alarmed at first but then, as the darkness washed over her, she realized that it was at least overtaking the pain in her head. And in that moment, that was the only thing she cared about.

She fell to the floor and in her last moments before going under, she heard Frank speaking again. She focused on that—on Frank's voice. In the end, he'd been there for her and that made it a bit easier to give in to that waiting darkness.

CHAPTER THIRTY

Ava opened her eyes and saw roses.

She was laying on her back with something soft beneath her. The roses were directly in front of her, as if greeting her back to the world of the awake and living. Her head was itching fiercely and when she lifted her hand to scratch it, she stopped short. There were stitches along the side of her head and she could feel swelling and tenderness there.

She remembered the glass being broken across her head, could remember Spurlock kicking her, could remember Frank coming in through—

"Mommy?"

She turned her head to the right and saw Jeffrey sitting in a chair. Seeing the chair, the featureless walls, and adding in the roses, she started to understand where she was. A hospital. Apparently, she'd blacked out in the Ash Lodge and—

What about Spurlock? she wondered, her heart already thrumming with panic and fear. *What about Frank?*

But for now, she had to remain clam. And Jeffrey being right there beside her helped. "Hey, kiddo," she said. She sat up, her ribs aching a bit and her head feeling like a concrete block. She got a better view of the very plain room and was reminded of why she loathed hospitals.

"Can I…can I hug you?" he asked.

"You'd better."

He came to her side and placed his arms around her. It did hurt her ribs a bit, but it was worth it.

"You're not here all alone, are you?" she asked.

"No. Grandpa and Mr. Frank are here, too. But Mr. Frank is downstairs talking to another cop and Grandpa is just outside, talking to a doctor."

"Do you know how long I've been here?"

"Not too long," Jeffrey said, breaking the hug. "Grandpa brought me in here this morning, when it was still dark outside. And we haven't had lunch yet, so it's still pretty early. Do you…do you want me to go get them?"

"No need," came Frank's voice from the doorway. "Thanks for looking over her, Jeffrey."

Jeffrey smiled and carefully sat down on the foot of the bed. Frank came to the bedside and took his spot. Without any hesitation at all, he reached out and took her hand.

"You scared the hell out of me," he said.

She nodded and said, "I'm sorry. I just…I don't get it. How did you even know to be there?"

Frank grinned and looked quickly over to Jeffrey. Ava got the gist of what he was trying to communicate and though she hated to send Jeffrey away after he'd sat so vigilantly by her bedside, she felt it was necessary.

"Jeffrey, can you go hang with your grandpa out in the hallway for a bit? Mr. Frank and I need to talk about grown-up stuff."

"Yeah, sure," he said. He seemed perfectly happy to oblige, maybe because he was simply glad that she was coherent and speaking.

She watched him go, struck with terror at the idea that she could have died last night, leaving him an orphan. Sure, her dad and Frank would help take care of him, but still…

"I was able to find you and that place," Frank said when Jeffrey was gone, "because I've been looking into Clarence's case, too."

"What?" she asked, not sure how to feel about it.

"When I realized about a month ago that this was going to be a crusade for you, I wanted to help. But I also knew that you held what happened to Clarence very close…very personally. So I did it without your knowing. Over the last few days, I'd been looking into real estate deals that had anything at all to do with Jim Spurlock. There were four that I found and when I learned that three of the four were businesses that had been closed down, I started scouting them out. Funny enough…I was on my way to the furniture store last night when I saw you. I almost called out to you but…I don't know. I didn't think it was my place. I almost turned around, pretty sure where you were headed, but something told me not to. And then after you went in, I—"

"Thank you."

"Well, sure. I wasn't just going to let you wander in there and—"

"I don't mean that. I mean looking into it all. For not giving up on me and…"

She trailed off, feeling the pain in her head starting to flare up again.

"Yeah, your head was sort of nasty. The doc put twenty stitches in. He said you lost a lot of blood and the swelling is going to be bad."

"My goodness…and Jeffrey saw me like this?"

"Yeah, but he and your father both thought it looked great. A boxer's mentality, I guess. You've earned your scars and bruises, for sure. Do you want me to get the doctor? I'm sure they'll be able to give you something for the pain."

"Yes, that would be great. Thank you."

Frank nodded and walked to the door. Before he made his exit, though, he looked back at her. He simply looked at her for a moment and then smiled.

"What?" she asked.

"I love you, Ava. And so long as you'll have me, I'm not going anywhere—despite what my attitude over the last few days might have said."

She tried to return it, to tell him that she loved him, too. But the emotion of it lodged the words in her throat and by the time she could form the words, Frank was out of the door The smile was still on his face and Ava wasn't sure she'd ever seen him looking so handsome.

***

Later that afternoon, after a nurse had come in to treat the wound and stitches on her forehead, Frank came back into the room. The smile on his face was even wider as he approached her bedside.

"The doctor says you can leave tomorrow. They think the blow might have scrambled your brain a bit, so they want to keep you overnight just to be safe."

"Oh," she said, slightly disappointed. "So then why are you smiling?"

"Because there's someone else here to see you."

Ava looked toward the door, fully expecting to see Jeffrey. He'd left a few hours ago to head back with her father so they could get something to eat and potentially come back later in the day. But it wasn't Jeffrey that stepped into the room. Instead, the smiling and somewhat uncertain face of Pawlowski came in through the doorway.

Pawlowski cringed when she saw Ava. She tried a smile, but it faltered a bit too easily. "My God. If you came out the *winner*, what about the loser?"

"The loser," Frank said, "was a man by the name of Jim Spurlock. And once he's out of the infirmary, he'll be spending the rest of his life in prison."

"Infirmary?" Pawlowski said.

Frank had shared it all with Ava earlier and though she didn't need to hear it again, Pawlowski seemed very interested.

"Broken wrist, fractured nose, two dislodged teeth, a black eye that had swollen almost entirely shut," Frank said. "And all I did was shoot the poor bastard."

Ava didn't comment. She didn't want Spurlock's capture to come off as a punchline or comedic afterthought. Honestly, she still hadn't properly processed the fact that he'd been caught—that the man that had killed her husband was officially off the streets.

She knew he'd be proud of her. And that suddenly seemed like one of the most important parts of the entire journey.

"So how long are you out of commission?" Pawlowski asked. "I had a partner for all of two days and look at what happened."

Ava felt a pang of awkwardness as she mentioned their partnership, but Frank waved it away as soon as he saw it cross her face. "Pawlowski and me already talked about it. I know you impressed Captain Miller. And maybe even Pawlowski, too."

"Maybe a little," Pawlowski said, grinning.

"If it works, it works," Frank said. "And with you in another precinct, maybe it would makes things easier on us. That is, if you'll still have me."

"I'll still have you," Ava said, reaching out for his hand. Frank leaned in and kissed her on the corner of the mouth.

"I just got here," Pawlowski said. "Are you two really going to make me leave already?"

They all laughed at this, missing the sound of Jeffrey and Roosevelt coming into the room. "What's funny?" Roosevelt asked.

"Nothing much," Frank said.

"Just Wimbly and me fighting over your daughter, sir," Pawlowski said.

Roosevelt looked at his daughter as Jeffrey climbed up in bed with her. The smile he gave her made Ava feel a surge of love that she hadn't felt from him since her final few times in a boxing ring, studying under him.

"Yeah," he said, not looking away from her. "She's certainly one worth fighting for, ain't she?"

Unable to take the emotional rollercoaster of it all, Ava turned her attention to Pawlowski, asking what she'd been doing ever since they'd officially booked Fairfax. And as Pawlowski filled her in, Ava allowed herself to appreciate the moment. While she lay in a hospital bed with stitches in her head and the knowledge that Clarence's killer was going to prison, a perfect presentation of her life was in the room with her.

Her father, who'd raised her most of his life without a mother or mother-figure present. Her son, who had kept her sane on the nights Clarence had worked late and then in the days immediately following his death. Of course, there was Frank—a hopeful picture of her present and a promising future. Pawlowski also stood in the path of her future, a shining beacon of what a career might be like away from the precinct Clarence had ruled for so long, in a new office space where not everyone saw the shadow of her late husband trailing behind her.

And though she'd love him until she, too, was no longer breathing, she also knew he would expect her to move on. To move on and thrive.

With Spurlock now in prison, Ava felt that Clarence could truly be at rest now.

And she could, as well…no matter what the future might hold.

A page-turning and harrowing crime thriller featuring a brilliant and tortured FBI agent, the NICKY LYONS series is a riveting mystery, packed with non-stop action, suspense, twists and turns, revelations, and driven by a breakneck pace that will keep you flipping pages late into the night. Fans of Rachel Caine, Teresa Driscoll and Robert Dugoni are sure to fall in love.

Books #2- #5 in the series are now also available.

Blake Pierce

Blake Pierce is the USA Today bestselling author of the RILEY PAGE mystery series, which includes seventeen books. Blake Pierce is also the author of the MACKENZIE WHITE mystery series, comprising fourteen books; of the AVERY BLACK mystery series, comprising six books; of the KERI LOCKE mystery series, comprising five books; of the MAKING OF RILEY PAIGE mystery series, comprising six books; of the KATE WISE mystery series, comprising seven books; of the CHLOE FINE psychological suspense mystery, comprising six books; of the JESSIE HUNT psychological suspense thriller series, comprising twenty six books; of the AU PAIR psychological suspense thriller series, comprising three books; of the ZOE PRIME mystery series, comprising six books; of the ADELE SHARP mystery series, comprising sixteen books, of the EUROPEAN VOYAGE cozy mystery series, comprising six books; of the LAURA FROST FBI suspense thriller, comprising eleven books; of the ELLA DARK FBI suspense thriller, comprising fourteen books (and counting); of the A YEAR IN EUROPE cozy mystery series, comprising nine books, of the AVA GOLD mystery series, comprising six books (and counting); of the RACHEL GIFT mystery series, comprising ten books (and counting); of the VALERIE LAW mystery series, comprising nine books (and counting); of the PAIGE KING mystery series, comprising eight books (and counting); of the MAY MOORE mystery series, comprising eleven books (and counting); the CORA SHIELDS mystery series, comprising five books (and counting); of the NICKY LYONS mystery series, comprising five books (and counting), and of the new CAMI LARK mystery series, comprising five books (and counting).

An avid reader and lifelong fan of the mystery and thriller genres, Blake loves to hear from you, so please feel free to visit www.blakepierceauthor.com to learn more and stay in touch.

BOOKS BY BLAKE PIERCE

CAMI LARK MYSTERY SERIES
JUST ME (Book #1)
JUST OUTSIDE (Book #2)
JUST RIGHT (Book #3)
JUST FORGET (Book #4)
JUST ONCE (Book #5)

NICKY LYONS MYSTERY SERIES
ALL MINE (Book #1)
ALL HIS (Book #2)
ALL HE SEES (Book #3)
ALL ALONE (Book #4)
ALL FOR ONE (Book #5)

CORA SHIELDS MYSTERY SERIES
UNDONE (Book #1)
UNWANTED (Book #2)
UNHINGED (Book #3)
UNSAID (Book #4)
UNGLUED (Book #5)

MAY MOORE SUSPENSE THRILLER
NEVER RUN (Book #1)
NEVER TELL (Book #2)
NEVER LIVE (Book #3)
NEVER HIDE (Book #4)
NEVER FORGIVE (Book #5)
NEVER AGAIN (Book #6)
NEVER LOOK BACK (Book #7)
NEVER FORGET (Book #8)
NEVER LET GO (Book #9)
NEVER PRETEND (Book #10)
NEVER HESITATE (Book #11)

PAIGE KING MYSTERY SERIES
THE GIRL HE PINED (Book #1)
THE GIRL HE CHOSE (Book #2)
THE GIRL HE TOOK (Book #3)
THE GIRL HE WISHED (Book #4)
THE GIRL HE CROWNED (Book #5)
THE GIRL HE WATCHED (Book #6)
THE GIRL HE WANTED (Book #7)
THE GIRL HE CLAIMED (Book #8)

VALERIE LAW MYSTERY SERIES
NO MERCY (Book #1)
NO PITY (Book #2)
NO FEAR (Book #3)
NO SLEEP (Book #4)
NO QUARTER (Book #5)
NO CHANCE (Book #6)
NO REFUGE (Book #7)
NO GRACE (Book #8)
NO ESCAPE (Book #9)

RACHEL GIFT MYSTERY SERIES
HER LAST WISH (Book #1)
HER LAST CHANCE (Book #2)
HER LAST HOPE (Book #3)
HER LAST FEAR (Book #4)
HER LAST CHOICE (Book #5)
HER LAST BREATH (Book #6)
HER LAST MISTAKE (Book #7)
HER LAST DESIRE (Book #8)
HER LAST REGRET (Book #9)
HER LAST HOUR (Book #10)

AVA GOLD MYSTERY SERIES
CITY OF PREY (Book #1)
CITY OF FEAR (Book #2)
CITY OF BONES (Book #3)
CITY OF GHOSTS (Book #4)
CITY OF DEATH (Book #5)
CITY OF VICE (Book #6)

A YEAR IN EUROPE
A MURDER IN PARIS (Book #1)
DEATH IN FLORENCE (Book #2)
VENGEANCE IN VIENNA (Book #3)
A FATALITY IN SPAIN (Book #4)

ELLA DARK FBI SUSPENSE THRILLER
GIRL, ALONE (Book #1)
GIRL, TAKEN (Book #2)
GIRL, HUNTED (Book #3)
GIRL, SILENCED (Book #4)
GIRL, VANISHED (Book 5)
GIRL ERASED (Book #6)
GIRL, FORSAKEN (Book #7)
GIRL, TRAPPED (Book #8)
GIRL, EXPENDABLE (Book #9)
GIRL, ESCAPED (Book #10)
GIRL, HIS (Book #11)
GIRL, LURED (Book #12)
GIRL, MISSING (Book #13)
GIRL, UNKNOWN (Book #14)

LAURA FROST FBI SUSPENSE THRILLER
ALREADY GONE (Book #1)
ALREADY SEEN (Book #2)
ALREADY TRAPPED (Book #3)
ALREADY MISSING (Book #4)
ALREADY DEAD (Book #5)
ALREADY TAKEN (Book #6)
ALREADY CHOSEN (Book #7)
ALREADY LOST (Book #8)
ALREADY HIS (Book #9)
ALREADY LURED (Book #10)
ALREADY COLD (Book #11)

EUROPEAN VOYAGE COZY MYSTERY SERIES
MURDER (AND BAKLAVA) (Book #1)
DEATH (AND APPLE STRUDEL) (Book #2)
CRIME (AND LAGER) (Book #3)

MISFORTUNE (AND GOUDA) (Book #4)
CALAMITY (AND A DANISH) (Book #5)
MAYHEM (AND HERRING) (Book #6)

ADELE SHARP MYSTERY SERIES
LEFT TO DIE (Book #1)
LEFT TO RUN (Book #2)
LEFT TO HIDE (Book #3)
LEFT TO KILL (Book #4)
LEFT TO MURDER (Book #5)
LEFT TO ENVY (Book #6)
LEFT TO LAPSE (Book #7)
LEFT TO VANISH (Book #8)
LEFT TO HUNT (Book #9)
LEFT TO FEAR (Book #10)
LEFT TO PREY (Book #11)
LEFT TO LURE (Book #12)
LEFT TO CRAVE (Book #13)
LEFT TO LOATHE (Book #14)
LEFT TO HARM (Book #15)
LEFT TO RUIN (Book #16)

THE AU PAIR SERIES
ALMOST GONE (Book#1)
ALMOST LOST (Book #2)
ALMOST DEAD (Book #3)

ZOE PRIME MYSTERY SERIES
FACE OF DEATH (Book#1)
FACE OF MURDER (Book #2)
FACE OF FEAR (Book #3)
FACE OF MADNESS (Book #4)
FACE OF FURY (Book #5)
FACE OF DARKNESS (Book #6)

A JESSIE HUNT PSYCHOLOGICAL SUSPENSE SERIES
THE PERFECT WIFE (Book #1)
THE PERFECT BLOCK (Book #2)
THE PERFECT HOUSE (Book #3)
THE PERFECT SMILE (Book #4)

THE PERFECT LIE (Book #5)
THE PERFECT LOOK (Book #6)
THE PERFECT AFFAIR (Book #7)
THE PERFECT ALIBI (Book #8)
THE PERFECT NEIGHBOR (Book #9)
THE PERFECT DISGUISE (Book #10)
THE PERFECT SECRET (Book #11)
THE PERFECT FAÇADE (Book #12)
THE PERFECT IMPRESSION (Book #13)
THE PERFECT DECEIT (Book #14)
THE PERFECT MISTRESS (Book #15)
THE PERFECT IMAGE (Book #16)
THE PERFECT VEIL (Book #17)
THE PERFECT INDISCRETION (Book #18)
THE PERFECT RUMOR (Book #19)
THE PERFECT COUPLE (Book #20)
THE PERFECT MURDER (Book #21)
THE PERFECT HUSBAND (Book #22)
THE PERFECT SCANDAL (Book #23)
THE PERFECT MASK (Book #24)
THE PERFECT RUSE (Book #25)
THE PERFECT VENEER (Book #26)

CHLOE FINE PSYCHOLOGICAL SUSPENSE SERIES
NEXT DOOR (Book #1)
A NEIGHBOR'S LIE (Book #2)
CUL DE SAC (Book #3)
SILENT NEIGHBOR (Book #4)
HOMECOMING (Book #5)
TINTED WINDOWS (Book #6)

KATE WISE MYSTERY SERIES
IF SHE KNEW (Book #1)
IF SHE SAW (Book #2)
IF SHE RAN (Book #3)
IF SHE HID (Book #4)
IF SHE FLED (Book #5)
IF SHE FEARED (Book #6)
IF SHE HEARD (Book #7)

BEFORE HE STALKS (Book #13)
BEFORE HE HARMS (Book #14)

AVERY BLACK MYSTERY SERIES
CAUSE TO KILL (Book #1)
CAUSE TO RUN (Book #2)
CAUSE TO HIDE (Book #3)
CAUSE TO FEAR (Book #4)
CAUSE TO SAVE (Book #5)
CAUSE TO DREAD (Book #6)

KERI LOCKE MYSTERY SERIES
A TRACE OF DEATH (Book #1)
A TRACE OF MURDER (Book #2)
A TRACE OF VICE (Book #3)
A TRACE OF CRIME (Book #4)
A TRACE OF HOPE (Book #5)